Discernment II: Touched

By
LACY SEREDUK

DEDICATION

To My Children-
Since you all want to be on a cover, I have to write more
books. I hope you enjoy and that I don't give you
nightmares.

To All Other Adult Sufferers-
May you find a way to live with your disorder and never
give up the fight.

ACKNOWLEDGMENTS

This book is based on real events, real night terrors, real nightmares, and enjoys a lot of fiction. Names of real people, living and dead, have been changed and, to honor the deceased, their relationship to me and the manner in which they passed have also been changed.

An enormous thank you is owed to my husband for holding me up when I felt beaten down, for cuddling me when I cried, not begrudging the night light, and for not running as fast as you could, in the other direction, when you realized just what a life with someone like me is like.

A big thank you to my ex-husband, James, for designing the cover; again. And, thank you to my cousin Noel, for your insights and assistance with the whole process.

1
TWENTY-SIX YEARS AGO

Laughing and grinning with my friends, two sisters that lived down the street, we were standing with our mothers in their living room. While I knew that I was supposed to be a model child, seen and unheard, I couldn't help but engage in the conspiratorial giggling as we were about to begin our very first sleepover. My mother and Ms. Blockwell were discussing the rules and the various information necessary for me to stay over. Ms. Blockwell nodded her head after each item was listed by my mother. No caffeine, limited sugar, no Kool-Aid, not sweets after 7pm, no chocolate, no unsupervised swimming in the backyard pool, no movies over a PG rating, no PG movies with scary or disturbing elements, no sharing of beds or blankets, and I must be kept at least three feet from each of the girls at bedtime.

I could sense that Ms. Blockwell was tired already, wasn't enthused at the idea of having another kid to take care (being a single parent and all), and that she thought this list of rules and regulations were a little overboard. Nina, the younger of the girls, gave me a goofy face and then stuck her tongue out at me as she hid behind her mother's back. I laughed a little too loudly at this playful, five year old and was immediately reprimanded by the downward slanted gaze of both mothers, chatting above me.

The parley ended with my mother giving Ms. Blockwell a piece of paper with her name, phone number, and address as well as a reminder that, should anything occur, she will be right there to pick me up. I was grateful to my mother for not mentioning that I had bad dreams sometimes. I didn't want Ms. Blockwell to end our party before it even started. The older of the two, Jessie, knew and sort of understood about my bad dreams because she was seven and could understand those things. Nina said she understood but I knew she didn't because she told me once that her mom locked her dad outside and that he died on the front porch because he couldn't come in and eat. A seven year old would know that adults can go get food in town so that was just attention-talk.

Ms. Blockwell gave us a dinner of cut-up hot dogs with macaroni and cheese and a side of green beans. She had winked at me when she refilled my cup of Kool-Aid and everything was wonderful. After dinner, she shooed us outside to swim for a little bit before it got too dark. Jessie said it was because she was in the middle of learning about witch's black magic and she had a room full of books and she was learning how to raise the dead to bring back their dad. We played for a long time in the pool until Nina got mad that we wouldn't play her mermaid game and she started to cry. Ms. Blockwell yelled at us to come inside and watch a movie before bed so we had to get out and dry off.

As we settled in, on the living room floor, to watch The Labrynth, she brought us ice cream in bowls made out of pure chocolate. I was pretty sure this was going to be the best day of my entire life as I snuggled into my blankets and watched the troll man, in the movie, take the lady across the flatulating swamp.

~~~~

A gaunt-looking, old man, in military dress, was staring at a gravestone and singing. The words of his music seemed like they were supposed to be happy but there was sorrow in his cracking voice and I could tell he was crying. As I sat in the grass to his left, I played with the ends of the green blades in need of a mow. I wanted to look at him and see his face so that maybe I could find out why he was crying but I was too embarrassed. I just sat, gazing at the flowers on the grave in front of me and began to pick the little white flowers that grew out of the clover weeds and listened to his voice, broken with sobs.

> "And we're standin' right together now,
> In everything we do. And if my world should come apart,
> I'll still be lovin' you. 'Cause you mean everything to me
> And I'd do anything to have you stay forever.
> I'm an ordinary man, but I feel like I could do anything in the world
> When I look at you girl…"

At that, something inside of the old man seemed to break and he collapsed to his knees in front of the grave stone. His voice tried to come out and continue his song but it was strangled in his throat. I was so shaken at his sudden movement that I looked inquiringly at the side of his face. Unheeding me, he raised his face toward heaven and released a painful sob. Even though I didn't know this old man, I could feel the tears start to sting my eyes and my chest began to hiccough with my own bubbling sobs.

As if my sympathetic state made him aware of me, he slowly lowered his head back toward the grave stone and began to turn it toward me. At first, I wanted to reach out and let him know that it was going to be okay and that he didn't have to cry but, the more his face turned to me, the faster my sympathy began to turn to panic. Immediately, I could see that there was something very wrong here. His left eye was missing from its socket and his wrinkled mouth had blood seeping over the bottom lip and smeared slightly across the pale skin around it.

My own eyes widened and my breath stopped in my chest. I didn't know if I should run or if I should stay still. I knew that you're not supposed to stare at people that are different than you but my gaze was locked on the blood beginning to drip and spill down his chin. His wrinkled and bony hand raised up from his side and began to point, menacingly, at my face. This action made me think that I had perhaps done something wrong and I wanted to assert my innocence to the poor man with whatever I could muster in my face because my mouth wouldn't form words. I looked up from his outstretched arm and back up into his face, traversing the bloodied chin with my eyes and seeing that, now, his nose had begun to release a pattering of red droplets. My eyes grew wider at this proximity to blood. I'd seen it before but only from scrapes and cuts and a bloody nose a kid had at school, once. I recognized the fear that was beginning to grip me and every vein in my body shouted orders to move, to get out of there, but my muscles wouldn't respond.

Rigidly paralyzed, in my spot on the grass, I raised my eyes further until I came to where his eyes should be. Two empty holes seemed to engulf me with their nothingness and everything in my mind was replaced by a single, high pitched scream. His hand rose to within inches of my face and the screaming got louder and louder. The bony finger with its soft and worn skin gently touched my cheek and a feeling of being hit really hard exploded through my head.

I began to flail my arms, to try to hit it away, only to find more fingers, more hands, gripping me around the shoulders, grabbing my feet in strong clenches. I closed my eyes as tightly as I could, wishing it would all go away, desperately trying to remember what Dorothy had done to get her back home safely but I couldn't move the memory out of its hiding place. I heard voices calling my name and a little girl crying asking someone to make it stop. A mixture of confusion and relief gave me enough courage to open my eyes again but the man was gone and so was the graveyard. A strange room and strange people met my eyes and I had to wipe the water out of them in order to see more clearly.

After a brief moment, I recognized the faces of Jessie and the crying Nina. The stern and exhausted face of the woman, whose iron grip bound my wrists in one hand and my feet in the other, finally found its place in my memory of faces and I knew that I was looking at their mother. My relief was so strong that I wanted to jump up and hug this woman for saving me from the scary old man but, still bound by her hands, I could only open my mouth and utter incoherent words.

"Are you okay, now?" Ms. Blockwell asked.

"Um, yeah; yeah I think so." I replied.

"Then get up, I'm taking you home. Don't worry about your things, I'll bring them tomorrow. Grab your pillow."

Confused, I did as I was told. On the way out to the car, I wondered what I had done to deserve this midnight banishment, what error in judgment I may have made that would warrant a ride home in the dark instead of a simple phone call to my mother in the morning. Ms. Blockwell didn't say anything on the short ride around the block to my house and I was too afraid to ask. I couldn't even get up the courage to ask why we were driving instead of just walking the few houses down that it would take.

Ms. Blockwell ushered me out of the back of the vehicle, in front of my own house, and led the way up to the front door. She rang the doorbell and gave three quick raps on the wood before crossing her arms in front of her. More afraid of what my mother would do once she learned of my apparent transgression than the obvious irritation of Ms. Blockwell, I tried to hide my small frame behind her as I held my pillow with both arms like a shield in front of me.

My mother opened the door but didn't look like she had been sleeping. She looked from Ms. Blockwell's angry face and down to mine. With a slight sigh, she stepped to the side and held the door open a little wider. She motioned for me to come forward and said, "Go on to bed. We'll talk in the morning." I did as I was told and moved quicker than usual because I didn't want to have to see my mother's face when Ms. Blockwell explained whatever it was that I had done. My embarrassment and sadness made the trip to sleep quick and the wetness of my pillow seemed soothing as I cried.

2

"Okay," I say, to Dr. Marie, as I settle myself onto the more comfortable couch in her office. "Here's what I have so far." I flip open my little, green notebook to the first 'diary' entry that had been assigned as my homework after my last visit. Dr. Marie's expectant gaze peered across her book-covered desk with easy attention.

"When I was a child," I hesitate as I felt a warm heat fill my cheeks.

"It's okay, Johanna, take your time. I'm not here to judge you and, remember, the point of this exercise is to try and help you get to the root of your fears. If we can do that, perhaps we can take some of their power away." Dr. Marie's smile is comforting and congenial so I think *Why not? We've come this far, might as well just do it.*

I start again:

"When I was a child, between the hazy and over-lapping ages of four and six, my mother had woken me from a screaming night terror. Sitting on my bed, she offered calmness and allowed a little compassion to be seen through her eyes. "Can you tell me what it was about, Johanna?"

Shaking and startled, at the sudden change of my surroundings and the feeling of being slapped into the light of reality from the darkness of that other world, I couldn't quite yet form the words. I could sense her exasperation growing, waiting for an answer, as she watched the tears begin to well in my eyes and the heaving of my bosom, trying to regain a steadiness to my breath. I knew that I must offer something or she would leave me again. Her hand would be pulled from my shoulder and the connection to empathy and the compassion of another human would be lost.

"I..." it was all I could offer as I desperately searched every corner of my memory to give detail to what had terrified me so badly. The only image left in my brain, the only image my psyche would allow me to associate with that horrific experience was this: row upon row of rainbow-colored, spiraled, candy suckers filled my vision at so close of range that there were only, maybe, five rows in total. Complete blackness sat beyond them and a circular sticker sat in the middle of each one, showing the face of a clown. It was, and would forever be, the guilty and embarrassed realization that the explanation of this image could not, in any way, relate just what I had found so terrifying about the dream. It would also be the complete and conclusive reason that I would never explain to anyone, in my entire life, just why I found myself so terrified of clowns. Like Proust with his cookies linked to feelings of home, I had clowns forever linked with the fight for my soul. But I knew that I couldn't tell her any of this.

My mother removed her hand from my shoulder, expression slightly glowering, with the understanding that no more information would come. And with that, the connection to the warmth of the world outside of myself was gone. Self-pity now rose up to overlap the ebbing fear and I cried. Not because I was afraid of the dark, but because I realized, at such a tender age, that I was more afraid of being alone and that that was exactly what was about to occur, because I had failed to provide some way for her to understand. I failed to form an inlet, to give some way of connecting, I failed so I must accept the consequences.

I watched my mother, tears flowing down my cheeks, as I sat shaking on my bed, while she crossed the room toward the door. With one last look of tired resignation, as she gazed back, I could see she looked older than she really was. Her years had passed faster than everyone else's and her vitality of youth had been wilting with each passing day. "Just change the channel." She said with an almost deference in her voice.

She turned the bedroom light off to leave me in the triangle of light from the bathroom door and then she went away."

I exhale a full sigh and realize I hadn't been breathing properly during my narrative. My ears have that tingling sensation that comes when you know you're close to passing out so I try to steady my breath before I speak. "That's all I have so far."

"I think that's great, Jo. That's a very good start. I know that might have been difficult for you but it's definitely a step in the right direction. When you think of your next entry, I want you to stay on this same track and try to remember the first times that you were afraid and what you felt afraid of, no matter how silly your adult mind tells you that they may be."

Ha! I think, *No matter how old my adult mind gets, they'll all be silly and terrifying which is probably why I don't remember many of them.* "Sure, okay." I say instead.

"Okay, I want you to keep everything that you write down in your notebook. Even if you don't read it here or even if you don't think there was enough detail, just leave it there. It may help you later. Do you still feel comfortable with once a month for meeting?"

"Mm-hm, I think it's been working pretty well, so far. The medicine seems to be working and I haven't had many episodes and my sleep schedule seems to be getting more on track."

Yeah, whatever, my brain interrupts, *If by more on track you mean a steady bedtime of after midnight or just lying there and listening (or wishing you could listen) to Clark breathe, sure, it's on track.*

"Good! That's very good. And have you tried the melatonin before bedtime, yet?" Dr. Marie can't seem to hide a little pride in her belief that I'm getting better.

"No, not yet. I'll admit that I just haven't remembered whenever I'm at the store but I'll try to do it this week so that I can report on it next month." Even mid-way through my sentence I know that saying I'll 'admit' something is just stupid to do. She's going to think there might be stuff that I won't admit.

"Okay, no problem. Small steps, hon. Do you have anything that you want to ask me? Any questions on anything or any feelings you wanna share?"

Ask her about the book! My inner-voice says.

It's too early to ask her about that. Besides, she'll probably bring it up when she thinks it's the right time. I reply.

Yeah, that or she's got it sitting there to torment you and see if you know what it is and how long it will take you to ask any questions about it.

I mutely determine that it is not the right time yet and brush the voices back to their respective corners so that I can reply to Dr. Marie, "Not quite yet. I've been reading some things and working out some thoughts and ideas. When I have a more formulated idea of what I might want to know, I'll let you know."

Dr. Marie just stares at me and I start to wonder if I messed up my words as they were coming out of my mouth. I'm not the most eloquent speaker in stressful situations. I do a quick replay of the audio, in my head, and determine that it all came out fine. So I add, "Thank you, though. I'm interested to hear your thoughts on a few things when I'm ready. Plus, I have been reading the material on meditation that you gave me and I think that's helping a little to clear my mind before I go to sleep- when I can go to sleep." *Was that good enough?* One of my inner voices adds.

"Okay, no problem. Let's plan on just checking in on those ideas when we meet again next month. As always, feel free to call the office if you ever need to see me or someone sooner or just have any questions. We're here for you, honey."

With that, Marie rose to show that it was time for me to leave. I don't really mind anyway because I'm running out of time to buy Clark a Christmas present and daylight's burning. I don't even really know where to start to buy him a 'first Christmas together' present but I do know that I have a few other errands tonight before I can get to the mall; and, hopefully, before they close. I've got an interview tomorrow and then dinner with Clark to exchange gifts.

You'd think I'd have learned my lesson about scheduling dinner after a potentially important work-related event but I couldn't bring myself to ask for a different appointment time with the hiring manager or ask Clark if we could pick a different day. *Besides,* I ask myself, *what would I tell him? I'm superstitious about ruining our relationship because a job opportunity needs to be scheduled that day? Right. I'm weird enough as it is. I don't need to go adding fuel to that fire.*

As I rise from my chair, I take one more, quick glance at the book on Dr. Marie's desk while her back is turned and she's opening the door. *It's still not time, we'll ask next time. Now, keys, phone, money, check!* With my mantra recited, I turn toward the door and head out to greet the falling snow in the parking lot.

3

"Okay, Miles, I'm out of the office. You busy?" I ask my nearest and dearest friend, as of late.

"Well, I was just about to call the President on the Bat-phone and explain how he could end famine but, for you, nah, I'm not busy."

"Great!" I say, letting his snarky comment slide. "I need your help."

"They're not locking you up, again, are they?"

"No, Miles, I need help picking something out for Clark for Christmas. I've thought of a hundred things and they all suck."

"Well, I'd bet he'd like any one of those hundred things." Miles replies.

It takes me a second to comprehend just what Miles was implying as I falter near the coffee shop kiosk at the entrance of the mall. "Miles, you're gross. Seriously, I need help. I've thought of a bunch of stuff but just don't know what to do. I need a man's perspective. Scratch that! I need a GENTLEman's perspective."

"Well, what good would I be if I couldn't help the great Jo-Jo save Christmas?" Even through the phone, I can hear the facetious smile that spreads across Miles' face.

"Well," I say, mimicking him, "Then get on the Bat-phone and ask the President because you're, well, the only friend I have that, well, knows anything about my relationship and you're also a dude."

"Okay, okay, okay! I get it. What are your options and where are you at. I'll see what I can do to help."

"Well, I'm at the mall... Sorry, that was an unintended well..."

"Addicting, isn't it."

I can't help but laugh a little at how quick Miles can be. "Yeah. So, anyway, I'm at the mall and there are tons of options. Nothing really seems like him, I'm pretty broke, and I wouldn't even know where to shop for a guy like Clark."

"What's the budget, Jo-Jo?"

"Okay, one: stop calling me Jo-Jo; that's a potato stick around these parts. And, two: let's say twenty dollars."

"What the hell's a potato stick? Is that supposed to be a potato on a stick? Or is it more like a potato cut into the shape of a stick? Do you eat it or do you fight with it? Are you feeling okay, Jo-Jo? Do we need to call the doc?"

"It's like a big French fry. Happy now?" My exasperation is starting to take over because the mall is going to close soon and I haven't even left the little coffee kiosk area yet. I can see the black-haired teenager, behind the counter, wrinkling her pierced nose and smiling at me as she, no doubt, laughs silently at my end of the conversation. I give her a half smile and roll my eyes a little as Miles continues on the phone.

"Okay, I'm happy now. But I do want to see one of these potato things you speak of."

"Sounds good. I'll mail you some and that should cover your Christmas."

"Well, I don't know about that but you could deliver them. That would be cool. Wait, do you eat them cold or warm? Is there, like, a special dip for them or are they meant to be eaten plain? I like dips, myself—"

"Miles! As entertaining as the dip to no dip conversation may be, we can continue it at another time when the mall is not about to close for the night. I now have 45 minutes to figure out what to buy, get home, wrap it, get out my interview clothes, and try to get to sleep for that interview tomorrow. I won't have a lot of time after my interview before I'm supposed to meet Clark for dinner and exchange our gifts."

In his most responsible, grown-up voice, Miles says, "Right. Sorry. I forgot about that. Down to business. How about a tie?"

"Oh for the love of Pete! You're no help at all!"

"Kidding, I was kidding. Calm down, Jo-Jo, before you blow a gasket." He pauses, for what I can only imagine would be, to create his next joke at my expense. "How about a handy-dandy tool set for his truck?"

"Nope, he's got one."

"Well, okay... I'm thinking automotive here. Seat covers?"

"As awful of an idea as that is, got 'em."

"Jumper cables?"

"Are you being serious right now?"

"I'm doing the best I can. Not like you gave me a lot of warning on this one."

I had to admit-- *There it is again, what are you hiding?... Okay, brain, how about this, I had to RECOGNIZE that Miles was right.* I hadn't given him any warning and I procrastinated until the last possible minute. Drumming up a little humility to my voice, I reply, "You're right. I didn't give you any warning and I'm sorry. I really thought I could come up with something but I'm a little out of practice." *Try a LOT out of practice*, my brain adds.

"Well, okay, I'm just gonna throw some stuff at ya and you let me know if anything sticks. Steering wheel cover?" I roll my eyes but let him continue. "Tow hitch? CDs? Autographed guitar by We Are The Hillbillies? Um, massage gift certificate?"

I say nothing but begin tapping my foot impatiently. I turn to the woman at the kiosk, hand her my debit card and point at the cheapest, biggest, regular coffee from the laminated menu and smile apologetically. The voice of Miles still drones on in my ear and I'm pretty sure that he's had more than his daily serving of Mountain Dew in the last hour alone, easy.

"New propane tank for a barbeque grill? Scented candles? A belly rub? A knitted, Christmas sweater? Socks? I don't care what anyone says, socks are great for Christmas. Um, chrome polish? Leather polish? A new hood ornament? Flood lights—"

Excited, I yell, "Miles, that's it!" The teenager behind the counter jumps and spills hot coffee on her hand. "I'm so sorry!" I say to her.

Confused, Miles asks, "Why are you sorry?"

"No, not you, the girl making the coffee..." Turning to the young lady, I say, "I'm sorry, I didn't mean to imply that you're a girl, I was just, um..." Thankfully, the girl didn't just toss the coffee in my face. She just laughs and wipes the pink marks from the hot coffee off of her hand.

The voice of Miles continues in my ear, "Well, you should be sorry because I'm not a girl."

"No, not you, Miles. I know you're not a girl and you're brilliant. A Christmas ornament would be the perfect gift. Something nice but not too clingy/needy/we'll-be-together-forever-ish and there's a Christmas store just up around the corner from where I'm at. It's perfect. A perfect idea."

"Well, glad to be of service, Jo-Jo. Now, if your crisis has been averted, I'd like to get back to my book."

With a smile that I know he'll hear, I say, "Please stop calling me that." I hang up and head to the Christmas shop to find something just ruggedly Clark-ish but cute enough to be endearing.

4

Returning home to my own, quiet little street, I survey the townhouses around me in the light of the lampposts. I rarely see any of my neighbors and tonight proves no different than usual. With only three days until Christmas and snow all over the lawns, I'm not surprised that no one wants to be out in the cold. The packed snow on the road is slick and icy so I ease the car slowly into my driveway and park.

Turning off the engine, I can see that there's an envelope taped to my front door before I shut off the headlights. It takes me a moment but I realize that it's probably a letter from my landlord, letting me know that I'm running out of time to come up with my rent. Not that there's anyone around to see it but I quickly turn off my headlights and let the darkness cover up the evidence of my ineptitude. Just three more days or so and I should get the deposit for the temp job I did last week. That coupled with whatever I can find to sell (which isn't much) will buy me another month and, hopefully, enough time to get a first paycheck if I'm offered a job tomorrow.

I open the car door and gather my belongings, pausing for a moment to watch my breath crystallize in the frigid air. My nose starts to tingle from the cold so I know it's time to go. Reaching over the center console, I grab the new bag that holds the nicest but cheapest pair of dress pants I could find and grab the bag from the Christmas shop. I make a mental note to try and remember to eat something before I go to bed since I've lost a few pounds in the last couple of months. Once the small, brown paper bag, containing Clark's present, is safely in my lap and the clothing bag is tucked under my arm, I do a double check before locking the car and heading inside, *Keys, phone, money, gift, new pants. Got it.* I shut the car door behind me and the clank seems almost too loud on the quiet street. Careful not to fall, I pick my way through the ankle deep snow up to my front door and nonchalantly remove the envelope; as if I knew it would be there, like I had been waiting for it.

My house is a little chilly since I turned the heat down to save money. So long as the pipes don't freeze, I can use extra blankets, since it's just me. The first thing on my to-do list is start a pot of coffee. Once that's going, I'll brave the spare bedroom that is supposed to be my office and see if I can't find some wrapping paper. The power must have gone off at some time today because the coffee pot is telling me that it's midnight. A quick check of my phone, as I set it on the kitchen counter, tells me that it's really only just after ten.

I reset the clock, accordingly, started a pot of coffee, and then head to the bedroom to set my alarm clock. Tomorrow is a big day and I don't want to be late for it, even though it's not scheduled until noon. As I flip on the light, I catch the outline of a woman in the corner but she disappears before my eyes can lock on her. Short black hair, African descent, dark skin, maybe a black hat, black clothes. *Oh great! Not tonight. Please don't let this happen tonight!*

As if the woman's sole purpose was to remind me to take my pill, I set the clock, grab the pill bottle, and pop one in my mouth without even finding a drink. I gag a little on the dry pill but it seemed prudent to take it right away so all I can do is screw my face up into a sour look and head to the other room in search of paper. I keep the door of the 'office' closed since I don't need to heat it and I hesitate a little before turning the handle. Without stepping forward, I let the door swing wide and bang against the crap stored against the wall and slightly behind it. Nothing jumps out, up, or otherwise so I flip the light on and survey the boxes piled everywhere. *Good, no ghosties. On to the task at hand*, someone in my head says.

About halfway of the moving out process from my old place, it dawned on me that I should label my boxes so half of what's in this room has titles but the other half is just guess work. Starting on my left, I look over each of the four boxes piled on my desk. None of them want to tell me their names so I take one down and open it. It's full of paperwork and old textbooks that I liked or couldn't sell from college. Not it.

The next box is the home of stuffed animals, snow globes wrapped in the comics from an old newspaper, and other various childhood things that I just don't really need any more. I take out my favorite bear and toss the box in the hall. I'll take it to donation tomorrow or the next day. A quick glance in the other two boxes shows writing supplies, notebooks, tape, everything that actually belongs with the desk. At least I was thinking when I put it there.

Moving to the wall, across from the door, I open the first boxes under the window. Nothing too promising so I move them aside. Under one of them, a box looks up at me and says his name is **HOLIDAY**, in Sharpie, and so is the one next to him. Perfect! Why I didn't think to write it on the side of the box is beyond me but I'll take it. Looking inside, I find no wrapping paper—not even birthday paper.

I hear the coffee pot beep at me from down the hall so I close up the two Holiday brothers and head to get a cup. The clock on the display says that it is now 10:23. I have to get my clothes out for tomorrow, take the tags off of the new pants, find my nice shoes (which are probably under the bed), relocate the folder with my resume copies from the bookshelf to the table, and go to sleep... hopefully.

Once everything is taken care of, I snuggle into my extra blankets and close my eyes against the shine of the bathroom light. Dr. Marie had given me pamphlets on Beginner's Meditation so I push everything from my brain and focus on only my breathing. *Crap, you forgot the Melatonin!* I open my eyes and give a little grunt at this realization that I forgot again but force myself to close them. *There's nothing to do about it now*, I reply to the thought, *So everybody just be quiet and let's breathe.*

~~~~

Sitting across from a very quiet older woman with wrinkles around her pursed lips and a decently good-looking and (obviously Irish) red-headed 50-something man, I smile politely as he says, "You certainly have some impressive skill sets here, Johanna. We're definitely looking for someone with your experience here at E&M. I see you've been doing some temp projects on the side and that's very cool. I do have a question, though. Now, can you tell me why you left your previous employer?"

Even though I'd practiced this answer a few times, the jumble and uncomfortable fidgeting in my head makes it difficult to concentrate and answer so I clear my throat a little to make sure I have control of how my voice is going to come out. "Erm-- Yes. I was informed by their HR department that one of the employees above me had mismanaged some financials and corporate made the decision to release everyone in an attempt to mitigate further damage. Their investigation has been wrapped up and I have a copy of an email that states that their investigation cleared me of any wrong-doing. I'm also awaiting a certified copy but I do have the print out if you would like to see it." I open my folder to pull out the copies I had made but am stopped by the quiet, older woman.

Her lips open as she speaks but the wrinkles don't move, not even a little bit, "That's quite alright, Ms. Parks. We're well aware of the whole debacle that occurred. My sister's nephew works in their Dallas office and, once he could speak of it, of course, told me all about it. I made some calls and your references assured us of your character."

"Oh, that's great," I can't help but give myself a little mental face-palm, *Stupid girl, it's not great, it's just and precisely as it should be.* I tuck the papers back into my folder and force myself to make eye contact with the woman. "I mean, that's great that you were able to get ahold of them and I appreciate that. I work very hard to maintain my character and that was a bit of a surprise when they let me in on what was going on."

"I'm sure it was," says Irish. "I think we've got all of our questions answered for the time being. Do you have anything that you'd like to ask us? About the position, the company, anything at all?"

"Actually, I do; just two questions." *'Are you single?'* My brain offers up a potential candidate for question number one and I have to lower my eyes to my binder in front of me, hoping to all that is holy in the universe that I don't blush. Recovering as fast as I can, I continue: "I was looking through the company's newsletter for this month and saw that there may be plans to open new locations in some of the surrounding cities. Would relocation to a new store be a potential for this position? I mean, as a requirement?"

Wrinkles leaned slightly back in her chair and met my eyes, "Potentially but not as a requirement. It could be requested that, the person filling this position, spend some time at a new store to train, set up, that kind of thing, but on a temporary basis. Opportunity to request permanent transfer will also be available but will depend on the company's current need, at that time."

"Okay, great. Now, the other question I had is really a two-part question. Do you know when you are hoping to have someone start and when you may have your final candidates chosen?"

Irish clears his throat loudly and closes his notebook in front of him as he says, "We're hoping to have our final decision made and an offer extended by the first of the new year. Should the candidate accept, the position would start with a one week training in Colorado, on the 10th and then in store starting the 18th. Does that work for you?"

"Yes, absolutely. The time frame sounds great and I could do that. Should I be selected, of course." I try to hide my excitement and remind myself that he was just asking for posterity. They both smile back at me and Wrinkles says she'll be in touch. Taking that as my queue to leave, I gather my things, shake their hands, and mentally kick myself for not being able to remember their names.

5

Feeling pretty good after my job interview, I texted Miles to let him know how it went. Having few friends, Miles had become my go-to person for sharing life information. We had 'met' online when I replied to a post he had made on a forum for night terrors. I've had friends in my life, sure, but never knew anyone that could really understand me the way that he could. I think I may have been outgoing, as a kid, but I'm not sure.

Living a life like mine tends to force people to be introverts. It's difficult to make friends because you have a hard time explaining why you slept through your lunch date, why you were messaging them at 3am, or why you didn't want to date their cousin. Making new friends is just as hard because, you know, at some point in time, a question will be asked or a particularly difficult night will happen and you'll have to tell them about it. Or not tell them and have them think you're hiding something. Other than the fact that Miles lived in another state, he'd been the best 'friend' to come along in a very long time. Macy, my college friend, knew about my disorder, first hand. She accepted it and let me feel normal. I tend to just expect people to drift away after a while; when the intrigue wanes. I'm pretty sure that Miles will stick around because he has the same problem making friends that I do.

Miles texted me back when I had reached my house and let me know that I was a shoe-in for the job and that they'd be crazy to pass me up. Even though neither one of us likes the word crazy, we tend to use it fairly freely in our conversations with one another. It's really nice to have someone that you know won't, and can't rightly, judge you for what you do or say. I sent him another message to let him know when I might know the result and then I texted Clark to ensure our plans were still in effect for dinner tonight. He responded right away, which was slightly unusual given his busy schedule, and said that he was planning on it. We were meeting at my favorite Italian restaurant at seven.

Even though I had slept long and hard the previous night, I felt exhausted and wanted a nap. I had stopped at a dollar store, on the way home from the interview, and picked up a small pack of wrapping paper, in the Christmas genre, so that I could wrap Clark's present. I decided on a game plan: 1. Call the landlord and let him that I know that I could make a partial payment now and to let him know when I would hear back about my interview to ease his tension over whether or not I could pay rent, 2. Take a short nap of maybe an hour or hour and a half, 3. Wrap Clark's little ornament, and then, 4. Get dressed and head out for dinner.

My texted conversation with Jerry, the landlord, went pleasant enough and he seemed to be understanding. I set the alarm on my phone and the second alarm on my clock to wake me up in one hour's time. I set my items on the counter, next to the coffee pot, and couldn't help the OCD in my head that said, '*Keys, phone, money, wrapping paper*'.

At 5:18pm, I decided to turn the alarms off and just get out of bed. I was hoping to get to nap until 5:30 so that I could show up to dinner, looking and feeling refreshed, but it just wasn't going to happen. Since I had the extra time, I decided to try the synthetic method of looking refreshed via coffee and makeup. I turned the pot back on, to reheat the coffee that was left over from this morning, and headed to the bathroom to find some make-up. I don't generally wear make-up but figured, with the extra time, and since I couldn't sleep, I'd just do it and put some on. I applied a little complexion stabilizer (that I'd bought on my cousin, Cassie's, recommendation) and it seemed to help a lot. I gained more of a 'fresh off the farm' rather than a 'fresh out of the slaughter house' look.

Once I had completed the traditional painting-of-the-face that is so common in our current society, I donned a black dress that, I hoped, was attractive but not too fancy. I didn't want to give the impression that I was expecting anything over the top and it's not like this Italian restaurant was particularly fancy anyway. I set my shoes by the front door and kept my slippers on. The sound of heels clacking in an otherwise empty house just makes me feel weird and pretentious. Besides, I didn't need the extra height that the shoes would add just to wrap up an ornament.

I found the tape and scissors in the box on top of my desk and brought them out into the dining room. I had left the bag from the dollar store on the table so I pulled out the wrapping paper and opened its package. Cute little Santa's elves stared up at me, holding candy canes, as I unfolded the paper onto the table. *Great! Only one sheet in the package. Better not screw it up*, I thought to myself. I grabbed my coffee cup, filled it up maybe a little too full, and picked up the brown paper sack from the counter.

Once seated, I took the little box out of the sack and set in on the table, just off to the right so that I had room to work with. I flipped the wrapping paper over, so that the design would show and not be inside out, and decided on a drink of coffee before my crafting would begin.

Now, my coffee pot is not expensive, it's not fancy, and it clearly doesn't have a brain. It heated the coffee to, what seemed, a near boiling point because it didn't realize that half a pot only requires half the heating. When I put that scalding substance to my lips and attempted to swallow the lava, my immediate and subconscious reaction was to get any and all liquid as far from my lips as possible before blisters set it. Not only did I spray coffee from my mouth all over the paper on the table, I also managed to jump a little as I did it and spill this cruel liquid all over my lap.

With thighs afire and paper ruined, I set the coffee cup down with both hands to prevent further damage. So much for a little black dress at dinner and holiday oriented wrapping paper. I cleaned up my mess, changed into a skirt and top, and went in search of the newspaper I had seen in the spare room. Once located, I saw that it was actually the comics section of a Sunday paper and I breathed a small sigh of relief. Fate might bully me from time to time but at least it wasn't a complete asshole. Had it been the stock exchange section, I might have felt compelled to go door to door in search of something better.

As soon as I had Clark's present wrapped and ready to go, I set it inside the brown paper bag and placed it near my shoes. Safely out of harm's way in case any more flying lava decided to spray around my dining room. I picked up my coffee cup and tentatively raised it to my lips in hopes of a quick drink, before I had to go brush my teeth and leave, only to find that it had become room temperature. A few quick gulps, a toothbrush in my mouth, an application of lip gloss, and I was out the door.

One slippered foot in the snow and I was right back in again. *Keys, phone, money, SHOES, gift. Now I'm ready.*

~~~~

Pulling into the parking lot of the restaurant, I spot Clark's truck and see that he's still inside of it. I momentarily panic and wonder if I'm late but a check of the clock on the dash tells me that I'm not. He either must have just arrived or decided to wait for me. *Or he's leaving*, the cynical voice in my head adds. I turn off the car and try not to look in his direction as I gather my things and open the door. As if he sensed that I had arrived, he turned off his own vehicle and opened the door, smiling.

"Hey beautiful, you look great!"

Blushing and hoping he can't tell in the darkness of the winter evening, I return his smile and say, "You look good, too. Have you been waiting long?"

"Nope, just a couple months, do I look older? But seriously, no, just enjoying the heater. Are you ready to go in?"

"Um, yeah but you should probably close your door first or it will be pretty cold in there when you leave."

He looks at me a little confused and then realizes that he'd left his truck door open while he absorbed the heat from the cab into his back. "Oh, right. Yeah, I don't want to be a popsicle on the way home." He turns and reaches behind the front seat and pulls out a large paper bag, much larger than my little brown sack in my hand. Instantly, I can feel my very soul crumbling with dread that his gift will be bigger and nicer than mine.

He closes the door, comes around to my side of my car, and offers me his arm. "Shall we?"

I loop my arm in his, giddy like an idiot, and we head inside the restaurant. Clark tells the host that we have a reservation under Dixon and we're lead to our table. Soft, Christmas music plays without words and the restaurant is decked out with boughs and wreaths, giving a comfortable but not overdone atmosphere. Little candles in colored glass holders are on every table and we're seated in front of the big windows, facing the patio.

We ordered drinks and an appetizer to share and I tried not to eye the large bag that he set covertly to his side, on the floor. The waiter left with our order and, Clark, with an almost bursting enthusiasm, gave me his best smile and lifted the bag off of the floor.

"So, I can't wait. I wanted to wait until later to give you your present but it's driving me crazy and I want to know if you like it."

"I'm sure I will," I say, a little surprised at his excitement. "Do you want yours, now, too? I'll just say, up front, I'm sorry if you don't like it. I wasn't sure what to get you but thought this would be good." I lift my own little brown bag from the floor and hold it in my lap.

"Sure, but I wanna go first." He says. Clark reaches inside the large bag and takes out a small, unwrapped ring box.

Woah, way too soon, buddy! My inner-voice says at it simultaneously recoils and smiles at the thought.

"Okay, so, I actually have two presents for you but this is the first one." He hands me the large bag, careful not to pass it over the candle in the middle of the table.

Clumsily, I take it and bring it down by my side so that I can see what was so heavy inside of it. A large, potted, cactus-looking thing makes my brow furrow until recognition registers and I realize it's an Aloe Vera plant. Surprised happiness replaces the confusion on my face and I give a little gasp as I take it out of the bag. "It's wonderful! Thank you so much! I love it!"

"Well, I noticed that you didn't have any plants in your house and, you kinda seem to get hurt a lot so, I thought it would be a good present for you." By the look on his face, I can tell that he's doing a little happy dance in his head over the success of his gift.

"Thank you, I really do love it. And, as awkward as it is to admit, I really could use one of these. I kind of burn myself a lot." I can't help but look at the pink skin on my hand from where the coffee slid over the brim of my cup during my earlier adventures. "Well, are you ready for yours?" I ask. I feel a little better now about giving him an ornament since he had just given me a plant.

"Well, I've got one more thing for you, real quick. Now, I don't want you to get too excited, it's not that great, but I think things have been going pretty well and I know that stuff for you has been kinda hard since we first started seeing each other. What I mean is, I had already been thinking about it and it just sort of seemed like a good time."

A little confused at just what he was getting at and wondering what was in the box or if the box was even for me, I slowly start to smile at him as he flounders in his explanations.

"Here, I'll just give it to you." Clark hands me the little box and I open it to find a regular house key inside. Even more confused, I look up into his face and he says, "So, what I was thinking was, you and your new plant could come and stay with me, if you wanted to. Well, and all your other stuff, too, I mean."

Speechless, I look from his face and back down at the key, then further down to the little brown paper bag in my lap that holds the little ferris wheel ornament with the year written on the bottom. I can feel the slight embarrassment and concern start to emanate from his side of the table and I know that I need to say something, to let him know it's all okay. I look back up into his sparkling blue eyes but all I can muster is to ask, "Are you serious?"

His amazing smile returns and he tilts his head just slightly forward as he knows that I want to say yes. He gives me a wink and replies, "As a heart attack."

6

Even though I know that my relationship with Clark has reached the point where I won't seem 'easy' if we spend the night together, I just couldn't bring myself to accept his invitation to stay over tonight. We had discussed the details of how moving in together would work, while we were at dinner, and everything seemed like a great idea. The timing couldn't have been better for the offer but I felt like I would be taking advantage of him all the same. I told him that I'd think it over and let him know soon. I also explained that I wanted to know how my job situation was going to be so that, if I did accept, he would know where I was financially and whether or not I'd be able to help pay the bill. With Christmas being Monday, I wouldn't likely hear about the job until mid-next week, at the earliest. Hopefully it wouldn't take too long.

With lots of kissing and holding hands in the freezing night air, we parted ways, outside the restaurant. I took my plant and key and he took his ornament. He didn't have a Christmas tree to hang it on (since it was just himself) but he said he was going to go out and buy a tree as soon as he could. With only days until Christmas, I didn't think he had much hope of accomplishing the task. He was planning on spending Christmas afternoon with his dad but we talked about meeting that night for a home cooked dinner. My place or his hadn't been decided.

When I got home, I felt a sort of sadness upon entering my cold and empty house. A quick glance around assured me that Clark was right. I didn't have any plants except the dead one in the kitchen windowsill. No matter how much I watered it, it wasn't going to come back to life so I decided it was time for it to go. I set my things in their usual place on the counter and took my new plant out of its bag. Testing the soil with my finger, I added a little water and vowed that I would take better care of the Aloe Vera, now to be known as George. I set him up on the coffee table so that he would have some light from the front window.

I had a lot to think over, regarding Clark's proposal, so I decided that tonight would be a rare beer night. I pulled out a Guinness, grabbed a notebook from the office box, and sat down on the couch to make some pro/con lists.

Reasons to live or not live with Clark:

I don't like living alone	I'm nuts
We could be in love	I'm dangerous (to him and me)
I don't have a lot of options	I see a shrink
He could keep me safe	I have no money
He's really sweet	Everybody leaves eventually
	His family wouldn't accept me
	I have nothing to offer
	He doesn't know about the Spirit Walkers
	What if I get worse?
	What if he can't handle it?

Three beers later, I realized that I forgot to take my pill and that it was getting very late. Buzzed and now exhausted, I closed up the notebook, pushed it to the side, and headed into the bedroom, deciding to skip the pill. The inner debate would have to wait until tomorrow.

~~~~

Smiling and laughing, the brown haired woman placed one hand on the counter of the brightly lit kitchen. "See, I told you that I could do whatever I wanted and you didn't believe me. Do you believe me now? Do you? Do you believe me now?" She spins around and levels her hazel eyes at my face, just a few feet from me. She lifts her hand and points the black, enameled butt of a chef's knife in my direction. "I told you and I told you. If I told you once... Ah-hah-hah-hah-ha!"

Even though I was leaning forward, with one hand placed on the kitchen's island counter, I could tell that we were about the same height and build. I knew that, in a fair fight, I might have a shot. Fear and panic fills my very pale face as I realize that this is not a fair fight. You're automatically at a loss when fighting with someone that has relieved themselves of all social considerations. Tears start to fall from my eyes and I raise my free hand and gently touch my cheek with my fingertips, never moving my eyes from her face.

In my silence, she continues her rant, "You thought I wouldn't do it, didn't you? Ah, come on-ha-ha-ha-ha! You thought I really wouldn't do it. I told you I would. But you weren't listening. You were just enjoying the river, watching the water, and you didn't give one shit about the bear behind you. Well, you know now don't you? Don't you!" Her maniacal laughter turned so swiftly to anger and rage that her eyes light up and she lunges toward me. So fast that I don't even have a chance to move out of her way.

The only movement I can make is to lower my hand from my cheek and place my palm out in a pointless attempt to stop her as she plunges the carving knife into my stomach. A burning pain explodes inside me and I can feel the skin tearing apart while my organs knot and churn. My eyes go wide and I feel myself hitting my knees on the tiled floor with a loud crack.

Opening my eyes, I see the woman sitting on the counter opposite me, still talking and laughing, gesticulating with yet another knife. As if she didn't even realize I had fainted, she continues her tirade, occasionally tapping the butt of the blade on the counter for emphasis. I'm woozy but coherent so I look down to survey the damage. My shirt and skirt are covered in blood and there is a small pool starting to form between my outstretched legs. I attempt to move and sit up but a strange, gyrating, almost grinding feeling from my insides unnerves me. Panic begins to set in as every move causes the grinding feeling to increase and sharp waves of pain emanate from my pelvis.

I look into the woman's face, hoping for answers, but I can't speak. She catches my movement and stops mid-sentence, "—Oh, you're awake now, good. It wasn't all that fun to talk without you. You're so witty, you have so much to add. What's that? You want to know something? Ha! You're having fun, aren't you! I know you are, you little devil." She squeals with laughter and jumps off of the countertop. Holding the enameled butt of the clean knife, she twists her finger tip over the edge until a small bead of bright red blood starts to form.

"I—" I try to speak but no real words will form and I don't really know what to say anyway. I want to scream for help but I feel so weak, I don't even think I could scream. I can feel my heart beating in my chest but it seems slower than it should be. The small pool of blood between my legs is growing into a puddle. Blood has started to seep across my skirt and has almost soaked it entirely. I look back at the woman as she begins to pace and realize, again, that there is no blood on the knife in her hand. The magnetic strip, behind her, that holds the other kitchen knives, shows that there is more than one empty space. More confused now than scared, I look back into her familiar eyes.

"See, little girl, the problem is that you don't think. You never- You don't think. You just go through life singing la-di-da-di-da-di and you don't think. But you're thinking now aren't you! Ha-ha! You are now, huh. I knew it! You're thinking, 'where's the other knife'. Am I right? I know I'm right. I'm always right. Come on, little girl, you know where the other knife is. You didn't think I'd just spend all that time while you were away sitting here, doing nothing, did ya?"

Thoughts fly through my mind at a speed so fast that I can't catch hold of any one in particular. Without examining the snippets, I realize that I'm dying. I try one more time to sit up, to gain some control of my body, and the wrenching feeling in my pelvis makes me gasp in pain and fresh blood comes out in a wave. Suddenly, I know. I know where the other knife went. Carefully and watching my attacker the entire time, I reach into my skirt and slowly feel along my wet, hot thigh. One centimeter at a time, I continue up, not wanting to find what I know that I will find, until the tip of my index finger feels something hard that does not belong there. Gathering what little strength I have, I gently slide my fingers around the knife's handle and pull.

A pain I've never felt before, spreads like wildfire up my spine and down my legs. Blood gushes out of the new wound and my heart beat slows even more. Gripping the blade but too weak to even lift it, I feel a complete exhaustion creeping over me. My breathing is difficult and my eyes don't want to stay open. As the woman laughs and laughs to the point of tears, I know that I'm dying. I feel one last beat before my eyes close my ears stop working and it's over.

Opening my eyes, I know that this must be the life after death. This is what happens to your soul when your body has died. I peer into the semi-darkness around me and try to discern just where I might be or what will happen next. After moments that seemed like minutes, I recognize my own living room. I'm sitting on the floor, in a crumpled heap, legs splayed out in front of me, hands resting on the hardwood floor.

More alert now, I lurch myself up into a sitting position and look more completely at my surroundings. *Oh thank god I'm not dead!* My inner-voice screams. *I'm not dead, I'm not dead, she didn't kill me!* With new life infused into my arms and hands, I grab my stomach and look down at where the first knife wound should be. My eyes open in horror and I begin to scream hysterically at the sight of all the blood.

7

After my screaming and fear stopped my brain and inner thoughts from working entirely, I slowly raised myself off of the floor and headed into my bathroom without turning on a single light. Completely on autopilot, I heated the water in the shower until my hand could hardly stand the outpouring. With the water hot enough to wash away sin, I climbed, fully clothed, into the tub. I sat there without thinking, watching the rivulets of red drain my tears away. Huddled with my knees to my chest and my hands gripping tightly to the life inside my body, I dozed with an exhaustion I hadn't yet ever known.

~~~~

Sometime later, I woke with a start, as cold water poured spidery tributaries down my face. A very large knocking sound was coming from somewhere in the house but I couldn't tell where or what it even was. Not being sure how I got here, I turn off the water and survey my soaking clothes as the knocking continues. I listen more intently but the knocking sound has stopped. As I lift my aching body from my seated position, I groan and wince while my muscles argue over the movement.

Peering out of the bathtub's enclosure, I see that there are no towels, hanging from prior use and so I must step out, wet and dripping, in search of one. I begin to strip in the tub, first removing my shirt and hanging it over the top of the shower door, when the knocking sound comes, once again.

"Just a minute" I try to say, but my voice comes out so soft that I can barely hear it myself. Knowing that they won't have heard me, I give in, give up, and continue to remove my skirt a little more slowly, easing my legs painfully out until I can hang the skirt up, as well. Once my dripping clothes have been set, I step out of the tub on wobbly legs. I falter at the door and wonder if I should even open it.

Standing in nothing but my underwear, the other residents of my brain come alive. *What if it's the neighbors? What if they come in, anyway, and find you standing here in nothing but your tightie-whities, how are you going to explain that?*

What if the neighbors called the cops? Or worse, what if that cop, that wants to lock you up,

*got a call about a woman screaming and now he's
going to take you down?*

What if it's Clark?

The last thought sticks with such force that I
turn the handle of the door without even so much
as a second thought to my partial nudity and I bolt
into my bedroom to grab my robe off the end of
my dresser. Quickly wrapping it around me, I run
to the front door and flip on the porch light. I turn
the handle and yank the door open, stopping it
with the side of my left foot so that only about a 15
inches of porch light can invade my entry way.
Completely expecting to see Clark, I feel let down
at the sight of a young man in his early twenties
with a piercing in his nose and a tattoo barely
visible from under his shirt collar.

"Yes?" I say, not hiding my hostility.

"Yo, man, what's up? Is Dave around?" he
asks as his red eyes, half-closed eyes peer passed
me and into the living room.

A feeling of relief that this is not a cop, THE
cop, forces a small expulsion of air from my throat.
"No, sorry, wrong house. And if there was a Dave
here, he'd be sleeping. But, there isn't, so best of
luck to you." I start to slowly inch the door back
closed to give him the semi-polite idea that it was
his queue to leave.

"Yeah, right." He says, with a laugh, "Dudes
prolly trippin balls, man. You sure he's not here?"

I can't help but wrinkle my face in disgust.
Not that I'm offended on an 'elder' level but I'm

definitely offended on a 'lady' level. How some people could raise their kids to speak to women without so much as a thought to their coarseness or baseness of language really irks me. "Wrong house," I say. "Probably wrong neighborhood, too. Good luck finding your friend."

"Aw, nah, man. He's not my friend. He's like my BROTHER, man. Dude and I got shit that go way back, ya know what I'm sayin'?"

"Yes, I get it. Wrong house."

"Naw, that's cool, that's cool. If you see 'im, though, will you tell 'im Nate-Dog is lookin' for 'im, man? I mean, that shit's fucked up! D'you hear what he did to Tracy? I mean F'ed to the D, man."

"Got it. If I see him, which I won't, I'll relay the message. Have a good night." With that, I shut the door in his face and locked it as loudly as I could. Both locks. My curiosity brought me to the window and I couldn't help but watch as he stood there, staring at the door for a few seconds. He finally seemed to get the point and walked down the path to the sidewalk. I shut the porch light off and return to my vigil, in front of the window.

The poor, drunk kid sits down, in front of my mailbox, in the snow, and lights a cigarette. *God, I want a cigarette right now, I'll bet he'd give me one.*

No, another voice responds, *We quit. We don't do that anymore.* My mouth begins to salivate at the thought as I watch him gazing, bleary-eyed, up and down the street.

The red-flag-bearing voice in my head pipes up, *Maybe I should call the cops...*
Are you crazy? We're not calling anybody except a taxi in a worst case scenario.

Nodding my head in agreement with the logic of the latter voice, I turn my focus back toward my living room. I don't want to turn on the light, in case it might bring him back, but I'm surprised to see no blood on my living room floor from the night's earlier events. As quiet as a ninja, I sneak over to the coffee pot and see that its empty of that awesome, life-giving fluid. Debating what to do, because my dry and exercised throat needs a drink, I spot the other nine, unopened Guiness bottles on the counter.

I weigh the pros and cons of drinking more tonight and decide, *Fuck it, what more could go wrong.* I pop the top on one and put two in the freezer to cool faster.; there's cold Corona in the fridge but I don't feel like them tonight. I return to the living room and open the blinds just a little bit more so that I can survey the street from a more comfortable position on the couch. Drinking my beer, I see the kid, gesturing up and down the road, as he talks on a lit-up cell phone. He lights a new cigarette with the cherry of the old one and tosses the used end into my yard.

Irritation overwhelms me and I rise from the couch to tell him to go pick that up but, the thought of venturing out into the cold night to confront a drunk or possibly drugged man, forces me to sit back down. I take a long swig from my beer and realize it's empty so I grab another one from the freezer. It's slightly colder than the first but definitely hasn't had time to properly chill. The lack of real heat in my house has provided drinkable temperatures so I just roll with it.

An undeniable buzz takes over as I watch the kid get up from the yard and walk, unsteadily, toward my front door. I rise myself and stand just in front of it, preparing my muscles to hold the line in case he tries to force himself inside. Instead, he just knocks and the noise makes me jump where I'm standing. Slowly, I count to three before I open the door.

"Yes?"

"Yeah, um, I don't know if you remember me, but, is Dave here?"

"No, I'm sorry, you've got the wrong house."

"Oh, right, yeah!" He laughs and I can't help but smile at his seeming good-nature. "So, I'm waitin' on my ride and they said that Dave lived here so is it cool if I just wait inside? It's super cold out there and," he reaches into the large pocket of his hoodie and pulls out a small silver container, "Look what I've got! This shit's like illegal and shit. Guaranteed to get your shit fucked UP! See, 'cause like, they dropped me off here so they're coming back to get me but they're gettin' tacos and shit and it's cold out there."

Mentally kicking myself for laughing, I find myself saying, "Fine, come on in. Just sit there on the couch and you can wait for your friends."

"Okay, cool, man. You're really cool. Thanks. Here, try this, it's like apples and shit." He hands me the flask so I politely take a quick swallow. Normally, I wouldn't have even opened the door but, tonight is not a normal night. I gag a little and cover my mouth with the arm of my robe and he continues. "So, did you hear about Tracy? That shit's JACKED! I can't believe he did that. Chicks a lady, man. Oh, dude, can I smoke? You want one? I got like ten in this pack. I'd totally share."

A little beyond buzzed now and enjoying the company, I look over at George, my new Aloe Vera, and responsibly say, "No, you can't smoke in here but I'd join you outside. Let me grab another beer and I'll get you a blanket."

8

My eyes are puffy and swollen and caked with so much gunk that I can barely open them. Daylight streams through the small slits and seems to light up my entire brain with a searing pain. "Oh god..." I groan as I try to lift myself up on the couch. A serious pain in my neck calls for attention so I slowly lift one arm to massage it. *What the hell did I do?* Taking slow, steady breaths, as I attempt to circumvent the nausea that seems to accompany any and all movement, I gently lower my feet onto the floor of my living room.

The cold air cools my lungs and throat but makes me desperately thirsty for something, anything, to drink. Before I can venture into the kitchen, I peel more of the gunk off of my eyes and realize that it's much too cold in here. I pull my robe tightly around me and survey the room. Six bottles of beer are on the coffee table, George has been upended and some of his earth has spilled out, the front door is slightly open, and a silver flask is poking out from under the edge of the couch.

"Oh man..." I put my forehead in my palm as I review the jumbled memories from last night. *Who was that woman?* I ask myself in my head. I look down at my stomach and am afraid to open the robe, knowing what I'll find and knowing that I don't want to see it. Slowly peeling away the front of my robe, I move my eyes downward, as if going too fast might reopen the wound I'm trying to find. My skin is unharmed but my stomach gurgles with threats of violence and I feel my throat tighten and think of the fastest route to any bathroom.

Swallowing hard, I breathe in through my nose and out through my mouth. I can smell the reek of cigarettes and old beer coming from my own mouth and my guts threaten to erupt, all over again. Rising slowly and unsteadily, I get to my feet and close the front door. Locking both locks, I press my forehead against the cold wood and just breathe. Once my insides quiet down again, I upright my Aloe Vera and scoop his dirt back into his pot. *I'm sorry about that*, I silently tell him. *Won't happen again.*

Moving to the kitchen, I set up the coffee pot and automatically feel a little more alive from the smell of the grounds as I scoop them into the filter. My mouth waters and I feel a sticky mucus that makes me want to spit. The thought of cold milk sounds like just the right cure so I pull the half gallon from the refrigerator and drink straight from the jug. More alert and feeling half back to human, my temple starts pounding and I realize that water and pain killer will be the next in line.

    With a glass and two pills procured from the cupboard, I sit down at the kitchen table and try to not think until they can take some effect. I realize that it's Saturday and that I have nothing to do, nowhere to be, and no plans. A quick glance at the time tells me that it's two in the afternoon. *I could call Clark and see what he's up to but that might seem a little clingy and desperate. Besides, he probably has a lot planned with visiting family and stuff. How much family does he even have?* I try to think back over every conversation, any little tidbit of information that might give me some idea but I can't find much. He just doesn't talk about himself or his family much. His family is probably like mine. I remember something he said about having a brother or maybe two brothers.. maybe it was a brother and a sister. His parents are divorced, as is the custom, and I know he's visiting his dad on Christmas day but I don't know about his mom.

    He probably doesn't talk about family because he knows that you don't have any and doesn't want to make you feel bad. This thought seems to make gravity stronger and I sink a little into my robe. My mom was planning on spending Christmas with my brother and his new family so my Christmas would be about the same as it had been for pretty much every other year. Just me and whatever friends didn't happen to have anything going on, either. Given my recent lack of friends, that meant just me. *At least I'll get Christmas dinner with Clark. That'll be nice. Maybe I'll tell him on Christmas that I'll move in and then we can start the new year together. A fresh start and a whole year.*

The pounding in my head is beginning to subside so I know that the pills are working. My dried undergarments are getting itchy so I decide to clean up the living room a little more and then take a shower. I can think about whether or not I want to risk moving in with Clark while I'm soaking my aching muscles. Seems like showers are the best way to think; as if the water gives clarity. Besides, my hair is a total disaster from not having shampooed or conditioned. I must have looked like a nut-job when that kid was here.

Everything cleaned up and bottles rinsed for recycle, I head to the bathroom. Just entering and seeing my crisp clothes, hanging over the shower door, gives me a chill and I remember the look in the woman's eyes as she told me about the other knife. I can feel my chest tighten and the first sign that tears could come if I don't change my thinking so I mentally brush it away and try to focus on the logistics of a shared living space. I remove my clothes from the shower and only half inspect them for any traces of the blood that was there before. I start the water to let it heat up as I carry yesterday's shirt and skirt to my laundry basket. A feeling mutely presents itself in my mind and I change direction for the kitchen, laundry still draped over my forearms like I'm bearing a dead body. I open the cupboard under the sink and put the clothes into the garbage can. A vague sense of guilt over the wastefulness of Americans prods at the back of my mind but I did what I felt I needed to do.

Back in the bathroom, I remove my robe and other garments and step into the shower. Just a quick one ought to be enough to help me relax a little and get my hair properly cleaned. I grab my sponge ball and semi-organic body wash and start to lather it up. Even though I'm already pretty clean, I want to wash the cigarette smell off of me and get back to smelling like flowers and all the regular smells that I associate with my cleanliness.

Images of Clark and his place fill my mind more than thoughts and I imagine what it might be like as I rub the soapy goodness over my legs. I begin to wonder what sharing a bedroom, every single night, might be like when I freeze and shivers run up my spine. A small trickle of blood has started down the inside of my right thigh and panic grows as it progresses toward my knee and I instantly think, *She put the knife back!*

Calm down! There's always a logical explanation. Just think. Use your brain. It could be one of those freak moments that all women get or it could be a cycle starting early. No reason to panic. I take a deep breath and finish rinsing the soap off of my body and the conditioner out of my hair. As good as it feels under the hot water, I just don't want to be in here anymore. *Let's go grocery shopping and see if we can't find some moving boxes.*

Great idea! I respond to myself.

Quickly shampooing and conditioning my hair, I run my fingers through it to help the water rinse out any remaining suds. My fingers slide through, from scalp to end, and a sickening, slithering feeling, on the back of my neck, makes my body tense up. Gently scraping my neck and pulling, I grasp the slimy thing and bring it around to inspect it.

A larger than usual collection of hair comes with my fingers. *Oh great, now my hair's falling out. What next?* Using my other hand, I reach back and pull all of my hair together into my palm. Sliding my grip down, over the mass, I reach the end and tighten my hold. Another large clump of hair comes out with it.

A little panic sets in as I add this clump to the previous and repeat the process. Only a little more comes out with the next two grips so I rinse my hair again, turn off the water, and get out of the tub. Dropping the handful into the trash my stomach lurches and I think, *Ick, that's gross!*

I wrap a towel around myself and survey the back of my head in the mirror. No areas of my scalp appear to have lost too much so I head out of the bathroom in search of a comb and some clothes.

While I get dressed in some warm clothes, I'm reminded by someone in my head that you'll 'catch your death' if you go out with we hair in the winter time but I don't really care. I need to find some boxes and get out of the house. Just the thought of standing in the bathroom and waiting for it to blow dry is creepy enough to warrant a hasty retreat. *Besides, the heater in the car will help dry it a little.*

After finding some socks, I work my feet into my winter boots and grab my things. *Keys, phone, money. Now, where to?* Stopping at the front door, I realize that I don't know where I'm going and am not sure who might have any boxes to spare.

The liquor store always has boxes and they'd be more apt to pull some out for you if you make a purchase. Even though I don't have a lot of money to spare, this thought gives me an idea. It is Christmas, after all, and Christmas is supposedly all about tradition.

Looking back around my living room, I take a mental note of where everything is in case it should decide to get up and move around in my absence. Feeling half confident that I would be able to recognize if a chair or cupboard had been moved from its current position, I look at my Aloe Vera and say, "Don't worry, George, I'll be back soon."

9

When in terms of Christmas, people usually associate it with rum in the eggnog, brandy in front of a fireplace with family, or even hot toddies (even though I firmly believe that nobody actually knows how to make them anymore). I don't know why but I've always associated Bloody Mary's with Christmas. I'm pretty sure that it's not the color scheme, either. I think there was someone that drank them and only came around for the holidays but I don't really have a clue. The majority of my memories from childhood aren't very clear and there certainly aren't a bunch of them, anyway.

I don't know if Clark drinks but I had stopped at the liquor store to pick up the necessities so that we could share in my annual tradition of having a glass after Christmas dinner. It had generally consisted of a steak I'd make for myself and a little bit of pasta but, this year, I would have company and I was excited about it. Not knowing if Clark actually drinks alcohol pointed out to me that I don't really know a whole about him. *Maybe moving in together wouldn't be a great idea but, if we didn't spend time together, I'd never learn. Besides, if it turned out to be a terrible idea, I didn't have a lot to pack.*

Entering back into the quiet seclusion of my little house, I kick my shoes off at the door, place my shopping bags on the couch, and immediately head for the thermostat. As far as winter days go, this one had decided to be one cold bitch. First dumping rain and then pounding shoppers with hail, the heavens had decided to punish anyone that failed to buy their presents early. Even though I had already bought the one present I was likely to buy this year, I wasn't exempt from the weather and had to drive home in soaked, freezing clothes. The cuffs of my pants had frozen into stiff sheets of cloth and I couldn't wait to get out of them and warm up.

Once I had set the thermostat as high as I could afford, I moved to the kitchen to make a pot of coffee. This proved to be a difficult task because my hands were stiff and shaking from the cold. Water dripped from my hair onto the filter, leaving perfect grey circles. Dancing up and down in my socks, I plead with the grounds to get into the filter and stop making a mess. Now ready for the water and still dancing foot to foot, I fill the carafe, and then stick my red fingers in the warm water from the faucet to thaw. As soon as feeling returns and I can bend them a little more freely, I finish setting up the coffee pot and head into the bedroom to change my wet pants.

"Johanna." A woman's voice sounds off to my left and I turn, expecting to see someone on the couch or near the front door, but there's no one there. I stop in the doorway to my bedroom and do a full circle. No voice, no people. *It must have just been in my head*, I tell myself. *It was probably just some thought or memory and you weren't paying attention and thought it was from outside your head. No big deal.*

Moving into the bedroom, I close the door behind me and do a quick check of the bathroom. Still no one. Without fully forming the thoughts, I ruminate on whether or not it would be considered crazy to just accept that you hear voices with little more than a shrug and a 'No big deal'. I half wonder if 'normal' people have these experiences and if they react the same way or if they freak out and think their house is haunted. Not being willing to check under the bed, I look into every other dark corner but find nothing.

This being sufficient evidence, I change into a warm and fuzzy pair of pajama pants. Well, they're not warm yet because my house is colder than an igloo but they will be soon. Grabbing the extra blanket off of my bed, I head back into the living room and curl up on the couch with my new purchases. A box of cereal, a bottle of medium-lower shelf vodka, a bottle of bloody mary mix (not enough money to splurge on just the ingredients so pre-made had to do), and a new can of coffee grounds. I still wasn't desperate enough to buy the cheap kind but I did pick one that would save me almost two dollars over my regular brand. I set my items on the coffee table and listen to the gurgling of the pot as it's finishing up.

I find that I'm actually really tired but didn't really do much during the day. I forgot to eat since I had slept through breakfast and lunch. *Truth be told,* I tell myself, *I probably consumed a day's calories just in the beer I drank last night.* My stomach gurgles in response, warning me not to even think of doing that again. I look at the bottle of vodka to see if it has anything to add but a sour taste fills my mouth and I assume that's clear enough. The coffee pot beeps at me so I uncover myself and get a new cup out of the cupboard.

Standing next to the pot, I carefully sip the steaming liquid when a light catches my eye. For some reason, the light in my 'office' is on. I can't remember having left in on but I must have gone in there for something during last night's hazy adventures. I put the cup on the counter so that I won't burn myself as I walk down the short hall. By habit, I pause outside the door and listen for sounds of any inhabitants in the room beyond but there's nothing but silence. I turn the handle gently and then swing the door wide. It bounces swiftly back toward me and I feel a surge of adrenaline at the half-formed thought that there may be someone behind the door.

Using both hands, I shove the door again, even harder. With equal force, it bangs and bounces back toward me and I jump backward. It clangs and wobbles as it hits the latch and one of my voices chastises, *There's a box behind the door, dummy.* I give a little laugh at my own silliness and push it gently again. The door floats toward the unseen box and comes to stop with another little wiggle. I shake my head, turn off the light, and then pull the door closed.

Returning down the hallway, I make a quick stop to recover my now not-so-steaming coffee and then head to my blankets on the couch. Realistically, I have tonight, tomorrow, and Christmas day to try and decide whether or not I'm going to accept Clark's offer. I think again over my current financial situation and try to weigh the pros and cons. Accepting would mean that I'm committing to a relationship with him. *Does he feel that way?*

I try to think back over the last several months and I think that he does. He hasn't mentioned other girls or other dates. Actually, he doesn't really talk much at all. *Most serial killers don't...*

Oh, knock it off. The odds of him being a serial killer are pretty slim. And, besides, don't they usually want innocent victims that would actually be afraid of death? What sense would it make to pick someone like me? I'd probably be better at coming up with torture ideas than he would.

Yeah, that's probably true...

I try to think over what else he could possibly gain from it but there really isn't much. I'm the one that would stand to gain more than he would and in a lot more ways. I love living by myself, having my own little space, but I also would like to have someone to talk to, someone to be there and ask me how my day went. *Maybe he feels the same way, after all, he is older than you.* There was a lot of potential truth to that thought so I explored what Clark's daily life must be like. Get up alone, go to work by himself, come home to an empty place, go to bed alone. Pretty standard evidence for wanting someone around.

-CLANG- The sound makes me jump and I spill coffee all over my lap and blankets. At least I had already drank half the cup but there was enough to do some damage. *What is with this day and getting wet?!* I lean forward and peer toward the kitchen to try and locate what had produced the sound. With no movement or further noise to guide me, I get up and head in to take a closer look. Everything seems to be in order and nothing really seems to have moved. *Yep, that's it. I'm saying yes. This place is starting to creep me out.*

10

Sitting up, in the dark, and leaning my back against a concrete wall, I can smell the cold earth beneath me. Very little light comes in through the 1' x .5' vent in the wall above me. A small ribbon of light is streaked, floating, across the wall on the other side of the room. My eyes haven't fully acquired their night vision so most things are still shrouded in total blackness. A woman is shouting from somewhere above me and I can hear a little kid, whining something, scared, but not loud enough to understand. I lean forward and listen more intently, closing my eyes to focus on the voices.

"What did I tell you about baby talk?! What did I tell you?" The sound of a loud, stinging, slap is followed by total silence.

A blubbering child, now crying gets a little louder as the sound comes closer. "But we don't wanna go down der. Pease, bubby's scared and I'm scared!"

The sound of a small body being knocked to the ground starts my blood pumping and I open my eyes, *I've got to find a way out of here to get to those kids*. The woman's voice interrupts further thought and I hold still to listen. "Back-talking now? You'll regret that this time, Missy!" A thump and a squeal follows quickly.

A dark spot covers the line of light across the room and I realize it's a door and I see the concrete stairs that lead up to it. Light fills the room and I see that I'm in an old, unused fruit cellar. I begin to wonder how I got here until I hear the little kid again, this time, I can tell it's a girl.

Her voice shakes and jitters with sobs, "Pease NO! Bubby's scared and I's scar-r-red!"

Briefly, I catch a glimpse of the abusive woman before she moves out of the doorway. Grey sweatpants, bare feet, overly large belly slipping out from under a zipped up sweatshirt. Her sagging breasts denote that there's no bra or under shirt and her pock-marked face is twisted in an ugly mockery of the child. "You don't wanna go? Pease? Maybe you should have thought of that before you got into nana's sweets." Her yellow teeth snarl as her greasy two-toned hair, streaked with grey, swings violently forward. She reaches down and, with an expensively manicured hand, yanks a barefoot and dirty little girl into the opening of the door.

"I- I'm sorry, we's SORRY!" Panic stops her sobs and her terrified eyes look up into the woman's face. " I said I was sorry. We not touch the sweets again! Please!"

The woman just laughs at her as she moves to her left. She uses the hand on the girl's shoulder to shove her into the doorway and onto the steps. Arms out and hands grasping, the girl just barely grabs ahold of the railing as she swings sideways into a half turn on the steps. I rise to my feet, trying to find words, something that I can do to stop this woman. With creeping panic, I realize that I can't take a step forward. Looking up at the doorway, I see a chubby faced but thin and crying little boy, with blonde hair and black eyes, is being yanked into the opening. I open my mouth but nothing comes out.

With more sarcasm and cruelty in her voice, the woman mocks the little girl's voice and says, "Now you and your BUBBY can have plenty of time to think about not doing it again. You filthy little pigs!" Even more violently than before, she uses both hands to lift the child, no more than four years old, off of his feet and pushes him straight forward through the doorway. His foot tries to catch a step on the way down but his ankle twists slightly and he goes face down, towards the bottom step. His blonde, unwashed head makes a sickening crack as it hits and my stomach turns and I heave.

The woman continues, "And if either of you so much as pisses, even a little, I'll make you wish you weren't never even born!" The little boy's body tumbles and rolls a foot or two across the floor, like a child-sized mannequin with movable arms. Unheeding the injury to the kid, the woman slams the door and leaves us in darkness.

The girl sits motionless, crying silently, and huddled just inches from her brother. Adrenaline courses through my veins and my body turns from stone to muscle; whatever spell that held me to that spot, now broken.

In three, angry, leaps, I cross the room, careful to avoid the injured child and shout, "Hey, you MONSTER! Why don't you try doing that to me!" I run up the concrete steps and slam my balled fist into the door. Blindly flailing with my left hand, I try to locate the door's handle but come up with nothing but dusty wood. I pound on the door, again, three times in my fury, and try the right side of the door for a handle. Again, there is nothing. No response from the woman, save her fading footsteps, makes my blood sizzle in my ears. "Open. The god. DAMNED. door. You dirty piece of SHIT! Open it NOW!" Still no sound from the woman but I hear a TV come on from somewhere inside the house and I pound more fiercely.

Sniffling behind me makes me pause and I hear the little girl say, "Bubby?" I turn and can see them in the grey near-darkness. The girl puts her hand, gently and sweetly on her brother's head. "Bubby? Bubby, iss'okay, now. She's gone."

The little boy starts to shake and I immediately think he's crying silently until I see that both of his legs are beginning to rigidly jump up and down. I'm jump down from the top step onto one in the middle of the short flight and spring onto the ground near the girl and her brother. Summoning all the calmness and caring in my soul, I say to her, "It's okay, honey, it's going to be okay. I'm here."

She either doesn't hear me or doesn't care. She moves her hand from the little boys head and places it on his back, between the shoulder blades. Gently massaging more than shaking, she says again, "Bubby? Iss'okay now." A look of confusion crosses her face and then a new kind of scared. I cross carefully around the writhing little boy and come to her side.

"Honey, let me look at him, okay?"

She withdraws her hand from his jerking back and looks at it. The light from the little vent above us shows that there is something dark covering her palm. Instantly, my stomach churns as a silent watcher in my head tells me that I know exactly what that is. I don't want to look but I have to. I turn my neck, eyes still on her hand, and angle my face toward the boy's, just on the edge of my vision. Slowly, I let my eyes move toward him and she starts to cry.

The face of the little boy is staring at me but there are no eyes in his sockets. I know, without thinking, that the black eyes I thought he had were not eyes at all. Just empty holes. His face is too pale in the dark grey light and his body jerks violently, completely. Chunks of half-chewed food lurches from his mouth as a dark stain spreads down across his forehead. One plump hand reaches toward me at an uncomfortable angle.

"Oh Jesus!" I can't help but jump up and away from him. The little girl scoots closer to his body and tries to lift him, struggling with the weight but his arm stays pointing at me. I fill my lungs with air through my open mouth as she continues her attempt to fully encompass him in her embrace and I can't help but think of a small child, trying to pick up a large cat or puppy. More vomit comes from his mouth as his otherwise rigid body fights her attempts. My eyes get wider and I can't move them from that tortured face. The pressure mounting in my lungs and chest explodes as I yell in an almost growl, "SOMEBODY HELP US! SOMEBODY?!! I have to get out of here! Please somebody open the door!"

The boy's body, back pressed against his sister's stomach as she tries, desperately to hold on to him, begins to lean forward on its own and moves slowly toward me. Now more terrified for myself than anything else, I back up a step and am petrified at the sight.

The little girl begins to coo with her sobs, "It's okay, Bubby. We're gonna be out of trouble soon and then we'll play and we can play your G.I. Joes dis time an' I won't make you play house. Does that sound fun?" A sob cuts her short and she starts again, "Do you wanna do that, Bubby?

Just tell me you wanna do that and we won't get in trouble no more."

Tears prickle at my eyes and I feel a shudder in my chest as I know my own sobs are about to begin. The boy's body begins to float in the air, coming closer but the little girl keeps her eyes on her arms, wrapped around nothing. With no real thoughts to grab a hold of, I hear myself saying, "Oh good lord, oh god no!" And then I yell again and turn toward the wall, "Somebody PLEASE! Get me out of here! I don't want to do this! I can't do this! Please, please let me out!"

I start pounding the soft part of my fists on the wall until I can feel the skin cracking and a wet slap following every stroke. Tears are burning my eyes and I can't see, can't think, and my nose begins to run down my lips. A choked sob erupts from my lips. My teeth, now sharper than they should be, rip at the edges of my mouth and I lower my head. A deep and fierce growl echoes in the small, underground space.

I feel a soft and tiny finger touch my face and fire explodes through my veins, ripping my face back upward toward the ceiling of this dark Hell. With all the power and force of my entire soul, I cry out through my tears, "MOOOMM!!"

11

"Please! Somebody let me out!" I bang against the wall in the darkness and my hands have become so numb that I can no longer feel the concrete. I open my hands and slap the wall with my palms and cry again, "Anybody?!"

A knocking sound startles me so much, in the otherwise silent room, that I fall backwards. During the seeming free-fall, I feel like I'm falling from too high up; much higher than the distance of my own height. I crash onto a hard floor, jarring my elbow with the landing. Blinking and unmoving, I lay there and listen as my eyes refocus on my surroundings. The knocking sound comes again and I see a couch in front of me; I look to my right but the little girl and her brother are gone.

The voice of a woman, panicked, comes to me through the wall, just beyond where the kids should have been, "If you don't open this door I'm going to break it down!" More banging follows the voice and I hear the sound of a metal doorknob turning. "I'm coming in and the cops are coming!" She shouts.

The wall to my right morphs into a window looking out onto a snow covered street and a small triangle of light grows from the door that hadn't been there. It slowly opens, almost tentatively, and the woman stays just out of view as she, no doubt, surveys the area for danger. Like ice water, the cold air hits me and I realize that I'm covered in sweat, half reclining on the hardwood floor of my own living room. Too shocked to move and now terrified of this person entering my house, I stay where I am and watch as the door opens completely. *Oh crap! I didn't lock the door! She said the cops are coming! What's going to happen to me? I have to say something, need to tell her that there is no danger.*

"I—It's okay! I'm okay, I'm by myself. There's a light switch, just inside the door. Just on the right.. I mean, it's on your left. I had an accident. You can come in."

A small hand with unpolished and long fingers reaches in around the frame, fumbling on the wall for a switch. She finds it and light floods the room, making my eyes burn. Her voice comes again from outside the house, "Okay, are you okay? I'm gonna come in now, alright?"

"Yeah, okay, I'm fine, that's fine." My mind begins to race, trying to find some way to explain just what was going on. How to make a normal person understand. I try to stand but the best I can do is to sit up. My palms make a sticky pop sound as they suction themselves off of the floor. I look at my hands and feel another rush of adrenaline and panic as I see they're covered in a light painting of blood. Wide eyed, I look back to the door and see that the woman has entered.

"Oh my gosh! Are you okay?" She takes a few steps quickly forward and then stops. Something familiar forces my brain to analyze her face and figure out just where she belongs in my memory. Her shoulder-length, auburn hair is free-flowing from under the hood of her bulky jacket. She almost looks like a little kid under the size of its mass but I can tell she's older, maybe my age. Black rimmed glasses, just a little too big for her face, glint in the light from the entry way as her wide eyes peer into the darkness of my house. Not seeing or sensing any danger, she turns her blue-green eyes on me and I see recognition flash through her face. "You're... I know you." She says.

"Yeah, do you live on my street?" I ask, still unable to place her.

She turns around and closes the front door, ignoring my question as she flips on more lights. I just sit and watch her crossing in front of me. As the living room light comes on, my eyes are drawn to a spot above her head, near the ceiling over the couch. Two bloody splatters have now adorned the wall. A mix of shame and embarrassment overcomes me and I drop my eyes, balling my hands into loose fists. The woman pays me no heed as she walks through my house like she'd been there a thousand times, flipping on lights and opening doors.

Returning to the living room, she looks down at me and smiles. "Why don't you wash your hands and I'll make you some coffee."

Falling into the easy familiarity and knowing that I know her somehow, I rise from the floor and head to the kitchen. My feet falter just slightly as the thought echoes in my head, *What if she's not really here?*

Well, another one answers, *there's not much I can really do about it if she isn't so might as well just roll with it.* I turn the water on, as I reach the sink, and let the cold wash away the blood. I hear her, off to my left, humming as she sets up the pot of coffee. I gently run my fingers over my hands and watch as the water turns a diluted red and empties down the drain. She comes up beside me and stops a few steps away, coffee pot in hand.

"Oh, I'm sorry, here." I say, as I move back a step or two. She eyes me a little cautiously but it fades as she moves forward and fills the carafe.

"Don't you worry about a thing. Why don't you go wrap up on the couch and I'll get this going. You're shivering and it's dying hot in here!"

Not having noticed the shivering before, it's now very obvious. I want to tell her that it's more likely a result of the adrenaline but I don't. Instead, I smile and attempt a little humor, "Well, it might not be so hot if you weren't dressed like an Eskimo. But thank you."

Her explosion of laughter startles me after spending so much time in the quiet. "You're probably right! Ha! I'll take it off in a minute and then I clean up that mess on your wall."

Confused, it takes me a minute to realize that she must have seen the marks from my hands above the couch. I smile sheepishly and return to the living room. She goes back through my house and turns off lights and closes doors. Even though the coffee pot hasn't finished brewing, she takes two mugs out of the cupboard and fills them evenly. Bringing them into the living room, she hands me one and sets hers down on the coffee table. Disappearing again into the kitchen while I sit and try to think of what to say, she emerges with a wet hand-towel.

She pulls her boots off with the toes of her feet and climbs up next to me to stand on my couch. I see that she actually has two towels in her hand; one wet and one dry. She wipes the mess with the wet one and cleans it up with the dry one. As she moves on to the second spot, I can't just sit anymore and I have to ask her, "I'm so sorry about this but I just can't remember where we've met. Do you live on my street?"

Looking down at me, her glasses slip down her nose while one hand remains on the wall. She presses her glasses up with the dry-towel hand and smiles as if I'd just told her a surprising and funny joke, "I'm Noel, silly. We're friends. Don't you remember?"

12

"Oh, right!" I say. Memories of my short lock up at West Regional Behavioral Hospital come back to me and I remember Noel clearly. We had first met in the 'Great Room' where she was reading. She had given me some information, based on her previous visits, into how the place was run and had even made it feel more like a stay in a counseling clinic and less like being temporarily remanded to the nuthouse. She had become a sort of friend and I felt like she was watching out for me. I never did ask her why she was there or what her story was but she didn't seem dangerous.

Noel climbs down from the couch and takes the towels into the kitchen. I can hear her washing and wringing them out. *Can I really trust that she's here?* I ask myself. *I mean, what are the odds that she could actually BE here?* I pause with my coffee cup half-way to my lips as the thought chimes in, *What if she's been stalking me?*

"How are you doin'? Are you feelin' better?" She asks as she returns from the kitchen and begins to remove her coat.

"Yeah, I think so. I mean, I'm sorry about this. Thank you for your help with the, um… With the wall." I want to ask again how she came to be here but I'm a little apprehensive about what her answer might be. I don't even know how one would apologize or properly thank a practical stranger bursting in and saving them from their own devils. My brain starts countless new conversation scenarios but none of them seem right.

"Hey, no problem. What are friends for, right?"

"Ha! Right." *How exactly would I know…* "So, are you like Superman, or something? Heard my cries from around the world?" *That was stupid. Why'd you say that?*

She laughs without cynicism and picks up her mug from the coffee table. Sitting down on the other end of the couch, she levels her pretty eyes, behind the frames, at mine. "No, I'm actually visiting my parents for Christmas. Well, it's really my dad and step-mom but they're my parents. I couldn't sleep so I went for a walk. They live just a few houses down. The blue-grey one on the corner? The Dawsons?"

Even though I know that I don't know any of my neighbors, I pretend to think politely for a moment and then give a little shake of my head.

She continues, "Oh, well, they only moved in this last spring so that's okay. They invited me, because it's Christmas, but I think they just did it to be polite. I'm a bit of a black sheep so there's not really much to talk about and even less to do. Especially when you can't sleep at night."

Perking up at this admission of another insomniac, I say, "That sucks. At least you get to visit a little, even if it is boring. Why can't you sleep at night?"

Holding her cup in both hands, she stops her gentle blowing on the surface and looks over at me, sheepishly, "Well, it's kinda silly, really."

She takes a sip of her coffee so I offer, "Sillier than saving someone from themselves in the middle of the night?" I hope that my partial admission of a ridiculous problem will help her feel more comfortable with sharing. I really want to know a lot more about this girl but am a little afraid to ask.

Her child-like voice alters her words a little as she tells me, "Sense you put it that way, I guess I may as well tell ya. I mean, after all, we were practically roomies." Her disarming, and completely innocent, grin makes me smile. "So, I actually left 'Death Regional' (as I like to call it) the day after you did. Dr. Sue... Did you have her or did you have Reinhold?"

"Dr. Sue." I nod with my reply.

"She was cool. Yeah, Dr. Sue said that my trouble with sleeping is due to a trauma endured during my early stages of young adult development and that I haven't learned to deal with and encompass that trauma." Her seeming recitation of the words makes the mute part of my brain tell my body do back up just a little bit. "I don't like sleeping at night, or in the dark, so I try to find other ways to make myself go to sleep. 'Cause, you know, you can't really be a member of society when culture says society takes place between 7am and 10pm."

"Oh, I hear ya there." I interject.

"So, well, I might as well just tell you. When I was, like, 13, I was into some silly stuff. Like trying to contact other worlds and stuff. I had candles lit in my bedroom because the 'rents went to bed pretty early and I was just having fun. Anyway, I had fallen asleep on the floor but woke up for some reason. I think there was a spirit trying to talk to me but I don't tell the doctors that, anymore. I sat there for a minute, just listening and stuff but I didn't hear anything. When I was finished trying to commune with ghosts and whatnot and I actually opened my eyes and woke up, I saw that something had knocked over some of the candles in my room. I wasn't trying to start a fire, it was a complete accident, but... Well, I couldn't see because of the smoke (the carpet was burning) and I knocked over other candles and the fire just spread. I had a candle on a bookcase and it just destroyed all of my favorite books. My dad was sleeping on the couch, downstairs, so he got out but my mom..."

"Oh, my gosh! I'm so sorry! That's... that must be just awful."

"Yeah, it can be hard; but, Dr. Sue says that, until the day comes that I can invent a time machine, I might as well just accept that it was an accident and move on."

"So, your mother didn't make it? How did you get out?"

"See, that there is why I have trouble sleeping. I don't think I was supposed to make it. Promise me something?"

"That depends on what it is but, if you're going to ask me never to repeat what you say, I can tell you that I have far weirder secrets that I'd be happy share."

Noel ponders the negotiation for a moment and then says, "Okay. I believe you. I don't see why they'd have locked up such a specimen of wholesome white bread as you if you didn't have your own crap to deal with." I just smile as she takes a sip of her coffee and I can't help but wonder, *Is she for real? I've got to find out her last name, or something, and see if this really happened.* She gets up from the couch and heads toward the coffee pot for a refill. On the way, she continues her story, "Okay, well, some of my school papers and books had fallen off of the dresser, in front of the doorway so it was hard to get that stuff out of my path to safety. Somehow, I got out into the hall, and then felt really sick and woozy; I sort of passed out, in front of my door but I'm pretty sure that I didn't lose consciousness. I didn't keep my room clean (like my mom told me to) and I had a crap-load of candles so there was a ton of smoke. My clothes were even on fire!" She lifts her shirt and turns so that I can see the scars of melted skin on her back before she sits back down on the couch.

"Oh jesus!" Is all I can think to say as memories of my own dreams of being on fire come back to me. I've never actually been on fire, in a real-world sense, but I like to think that I have a pretty good idea of what it would be like.

"Jesus has nothing to do with it, honey!" She shoots me a wry grin and finishes her story, "Laying in the hallway, I thought I saw a shadow, just standing on the landing, at the bottom of the stairs. Like, two and a half, three feet tall, and I thought it was a boy. I know that I didn't see him because there is no way for a little boy to have been in my house and it was most likely a result of the trauma I was enduring at the time. I passed out." *More rote influence from a shrink, good to know...* "Anyway, my dad pulled me down the stairs and then tried to go back up but, it was an old house and the fire was spreading. I've been told that he couldn't get to their bedroom. And, when I woke up, I saw my mom, screaming and on fire, fall down the stairs; she was all black when she hit the landing." She pauses, as if reliving this even in more detail than she'll share.

Slowly, I reach my hand toward her, to give her a comforting touch, but she withdraws quickly, and says, "A firefighter actually drug me out of the house. She died, I was sent to a 'hospital', and my dad remarried a year later." She inches just slightly further away and looks down into her mug.

The memory of her voice comes back to me, that moment that seems a life-time ago, when she touched my hand at West Regional during a group session, and I could only understand her words as saying, 'You can't take me, I don't wanna go."

14

After Noel's, what seemed to be, very honest sharing, I told her about my issues but tried to keep the descriptions light and not go into too much detail. I certainly didn't need her thinking that, people of my kind, had stolen the soul of her mother. We talked for hours and, the more I learned about her, the more I felt she was a sort of kindred spirit. Just someone looking for answers in a world that shuns questions.

She had seen another shadow person when she had broken up with her boyfriend during their senior year of high school. He had been emotionally unstable, doing drugs, and had threatened drastic measures before. She got in a car and left; only to find out later that he'd gone into the garage and hung himself. When she told me about the shadow person in the driveway, I decided to open up about my own experiences. The similarities were uncanny.

A grey light had begun to invade my living room and the sound of engines going passed became more frequent but we continued to talk and share. I told her more about myself and my childhood than anyone had ever known and she shared more about her experiences and how she had tried various ways of shutting down her body when it was time to sleep. She was terrified of creating another tragedy in her life so she had seeked out ways to just turn it all off. At one point, she brought up how she had found solicitude in a bottle; eyeing the bottle of vodka with a greedy stare.

I offered some (it was the least I could do for such companionship), and she accepted; provided there was ice or some other way to make the tonic bearable. We opened the bottle and our tongues became more free as the bottle became more empty. I found myself ruminating on the potential commonalities between my brain and that of serial killers and how it related to rage blackouts during childhood, she opened up about an uncle that may have taken too many liberties with a child that didn't know what 'bad touch' was, and we began to discuss how it seemed that we both had a great deal of stories relating to the amount of instability in every woman we'd ever come to known. It made perfect sense that a down-fall of female power in government, and even the world, could take place if these secrets of womankind were ever exposed.

~~~~

A knock at the door startles both of us and we, unconsciously jump closer to one another. She looks at me, black rims gleaming skeptically, "Were you expecting a visitor?"

"I don't even know what time it is!" Another quick knock sounds from the door and I get up. I make a detour to check out the time on the coffee pot and see that it's almost 7am. Returning across the living room, I give Noel a little shrug, and head to the front door. With my handle on the knob, I call out, "Who is it?"

"Hey, it's me... Clark." I hear from the other side.

A little relieved and a little happy, a voice pop up in my head, *How am I going to explain Noel? And why is he here, anyway?* I compose myself and unlock the door. The pain from gripping the doorknob makes me wince a little and I make a mental note to keep my hands out of view once the door is open. "Hi! Good morning. Um, come on in."

Clark smiles at me from the doorway and gently raises a hand with a coffee from some local drive-through place I'd never heard of. "I brought you a coffee. I didn't know if you'd be up but my client called and asked if I could come later when I was right around the corner from their place. It's pretty close to here so I thought I'd stop by. I tried to call but you didn't answer."

I smile sheepishly and realize that I've been blocking the doorway. I move slightly to the side and take the coffee, thankful that the damage is on the underpart of my hand. He smiles back and steps inside. His eyes meet Noel and he stops. "Oh, I'm sorry! I didn't realize you had company!"

Noel stands up and offers a hand in greeting. "It's okay, I was actually not going to stay long."

I close the door, behind me, without taking my eyes off of Noel and Clark, wondering if she's going to withdraw it quickly and zone out. Instead, she slips her hand in his and allows him to move it up and down, once. As Clark releases her hand, he says, "Nice to meet you, I'm Clark."

"I'm Noel. Nice to meet you, Clark."

"Um, here," he says, offering her his coffee. "I didn't know you'd be here and it's just black coffee but I haven't drank out of it yet. You can have it if you'd like."

Wow! My brain says. *Did I hit the jackpot of guys, or what?*

Noel laughs a little and shakes her head, "Oh, no! No, that's okay. I have already had my fill of coffee and, besides, it's about time I skidaddled on out of here. Let you two have some time together."

Clark smiles and withdraws the coffee. "More for me, I guess. So, I didn't see a car, do you live around here or need a ride? It's colder than a witches's... um, doorknob."

Noel and I both burst into laughter and coffee slops out of the little hole in my lid, splattering the floor. "Oh oops!" Still giggling, I say, "I'll be right back. Let me just go grab a towel."

The two share a laugh at my expense, this time and I hear Clark, as I head into the kitchen, "So, how do you two know each other?" My back instantly stiffens. I had done the upfront thing and told Clark about my short visit in West Regional after I had been let out but I didn't really mention Noel, not that I could remember, anyway. *Please don't sound crazy!* I silently beg.

"Oh, me and Johanna? We met a few months ago when we were both staying at the same place. I just happened to be walking down the street when we met up again, this morning. Pretty crazy, huh?"

I let a small exhale escape as I grab a fresh kitchen towel from the drawer and head back toward the living room as Clark replies, "Oh that's cool. So, do you live far?"

"Oh, I don't actually live 'round here; I'm just visiting my parents for the holidays. And, speaking of them, I'd better get going so that they don't start to wonder where I am. It was nice to meet you." Noel smiles sweetly and then grabs her big coat off of the back of a dining chair. As she's putting it on, she looks at me and says, "You gonna be okay, sweety?"

Mildly shocked at the sudden switch to endearing terms from someone I didn't really know very well, I just smiled and shook my head as I stood up from cleaning up the floor.

"Okay, well, if you need anything, just come get me. I'll stop by another time and check in." She gives me a smile with her white and perfect teeth and heads toward the door.
I felt the urge to hug and thank her but I didn't want Clark to ask questions. I just waited to see if she might hug me first but, instead, she stealthily stepped around me so we wouldn't touch. *What an odd girl,* I couldn't help but think. *Yeah, look who's talkin'.*

15

As the door closed behind Noel, Clark looks at mc with a slight sparkle in his eye. "Seems like a nice gal." He says, as he takes a seat on the couch, and I return his comment with a smile. "So, I've got some time to kill. Mind if I hang out?" He pats the couch next to him where my blankets are all bundled up.

"Well, I was going to just write my thesis on the global killer for human cancer but I suppose I could give you a few minutes." Grinning at him over my coffee cup, as I take a seat next to him.

"I don't want to interrupt something so important but I'm interested... What's the cure?"

"Returning to organics and only taking what we need from the Earth so that it can survive; and us with it." I say.

"Makes sense. Was she helping with your plan?"

"In a way, sort of. She was helping me understand that there are more out there, maybe, than I thought, that continue the harvest of the world's over-production." We sit in silence for a few minutes and what I don't explain is that I'm talking about the over-production of human souls, people that are created because natural selection has been out-bid. I ruminate for a minute on just what I'm trying to say but not say.

Nodding, he says, "I have noticed that there are some people that seem to think that they should breed just because they can. Don't get me wrong, I use' to be all for the pro-life argument. But, when girls I knew, family even, started having kids that they couldn't care for, emotionally or money-wise, I started thinking differently. There's all these people that have, like, five kids stuffed in a tiny apartment or trailer, living on food stamps, not paying taxes, and they have these giant tvs with cable television, and crap they don't need. I had this one friend, knew her since I was like seven..."

During Clark's story, my thoughts begin to overpower the audio of his voice. I want to tell him that my issue is not the number of babies being born, exactly, or the sheer population burst that we've seen in the last 20 years, but rather the number of people dying and how they're dying. It's a cycle. People are dying because we have too many people that no one takes care of when they're little and then they make more people and don't take care of them. All these people making people that have never been taught a value to human life. I can't bring myself to interrupt so I try to focus as he continues, "-I mean, well, anyway, I get why she wanted to have his baby, sort of, but I don't understand why she wouldn't take care of it..."

He gives me a quizzical look and I wonder if he knew I wasn't listening, "You're a girl, do you get it?" He looks mildly ashamed and I see a slight pinkness creep into his cheeks. "I don't mean THAT, what I mean is, as a woman, can you understand why someone would be so 'in love' with someone that they'd want to have their kid and then not want to actually take care of it?"

"Attention." Not having listened to the majority of his story, that's all I can come up with. I want to come clean, to acknowledge that I wasn't paying attention, but, he seems so earnest in his quest for information, that I judge it would be better to just pretend.

"That's what I was thinking," he says. "Drama and attention. If she really loved him, she'd have wanted to marry him. Instead, she just had a kid, hopped on the welfare wagon, and the sad part is that I think that might have been the whole goal in the first place! It's sad for the kids because the whole cycle just continues."

"Ha! That's exactly what had been going through my head!"

Clark sighs and shakes his head like he's trying to dislodge the negative thoughts. "Well, I should probably get going and let you get back to your day. My client's having a Christmas Eve party and they wanted me bright and early but then what do they do? Call me when they're supposed to be there already and tell me they're going to be late and that they'll need another hour or two. Really irritating. Just makes me want to tell them to fix their own problems if they can't respect my time. Especially on Christmas Eve when I have to drag my butt out of bed for it."

Looking at his face, I realize, for the first time, how tired he looks. I know that he works really hard but I'm always so caught up in his smile or his eyes that I never really paid attention. "I'm sorry. At least you didn't have to sit and wait by yourself..." *That's the best consolation you can come up with? Lame.*

He smiles and looks at me and the tiredness in his face seems to disappear. I can see something in his eyes; sweetness, caring, and maybe more. "Yep, you make it all worth it. Just a little bit of time and some coffee with you and I'll get up a few hours early any day."

Every thought in my brain dissipates and my body starts to tingle. My mind has ceased to be a solid mass of infinite electrodes but has, in a moment, turned completely to pudding and my mouth goes on auto-pilot, "I want to live with you."

Clark just gives a little laugh and leans over to place a short kiss on my lips, his goatee tickles slightly. "Better get packin' then, cupcake."

16

After I lock the door behind Clark, I know that I should check my email but I don't really want to. Miles will be really interested in everything that's been going on, since he seems to live vicariously through my life, but all I can think of is that I want to sleep. It's been a long and tormentful 'day'. The thought of sleep reminds me of taking my pill and I can't remember the last time I took it. Days and nights sort of meld together for me so my 'days' generally occur at night time. Even when I'm awake during the day, it's still associated with any hours prior to the next time that I sleep. I don't even know for sure what day it is today, other than Christmas Eve.

Putting the thoughts of anything and everything out of my head, I turn off the lights and curl up on the couch. The memory of Clark and that sweet little kiss sneaks back into my mind while I fidget with my toes to secure them under the end of my blanket. A subconscious smile creeps across my lips and I cover my head with the warmth of the blanket. That sinking feeling that comes before a good, deep sleep, overtakes me and I begin to dream of standing on a porch. Two, big dogs are wagging their tails, happily awaiting the food that I'm about to give them. One is mine and one is Clark's. His is a spotted, white strong looking dog; while mine is a black, beautiful German Shepherd. Whatever part of my brain that allows me to recall dreams, or maybe even have them at all, shuts down everything goes to darkness.

~~~~

Jumping up with a start, I look around the room. *Where am I? What just happened?* A knocking from behind me makes me turn my head, still perched upright on the couch. Groggily and croaking, I ask, "Who is it?"

Sounding more like a little kid than ever, I hear, "It's Noel. I'm just doing my rounds on the neighborhood watch and wanted to check in."

Smiling and a little more awake, I tell her, "Just a second." My stiff body tells me I've been sleeping in the same position for some time but the grey light outside is the same as when I fell asleep. "I'm coming." I say, as I limp toward the door. *Man, I'm getting old.* Opening the door, I see Noel in fresh clothes, hair curled, and glasses pushed up on the crown of her head. Reviewing the light make up on her face, it dawns on me that she's actually really pretty and that I probably look like garbage. Too embarrassed over how disheveled I must look to say anything, I just step to the side and motion for her to come in.

"So," She says, surveying the living room. "Have you been attacking the walls again? Don't tell me the sofa's been giving you grief." She eyes the messy blankets on the couch with a disgusted distrust.

I giggle and say, "No, everything is all good. Nobody has been acting out. I was actually just sleeping. Do you know what time it is?" Instead of going to check the time on the coffee pot, I just sit back down inside my blankets.

Mimicking an olde town crier, she says, "Yep, it's five o'clock and all is well!" She giggles to herself and takes off her big, puffy coat to reveal an obviously expensive brushed wool sweater dress. In the black of her clothes, she looks even tinier than usual. "So, that means it's dinner time and you can't spend Christmas eve in your pjs. Come on, get up, get dressed, and let's go."

Confusion furrows my brows as I try to search through my memories for any time that I may have agreed to dinner or that dinner might have even been mentioned. I fail to find anything meaningful and look up at her from my seated position. "You want to go get something to eat?"

"Yep, my treat. Well, my dad's treat, anyway. They're going to a party so he gave me some money and told me to be good. We can even go out for a breakfast dinner if you want, since you're just getting up for the day. But, come on, you need to get out of the house."

Finding no valid argument to contest this line of thinking, I just shrug and say, "Okay. Can I take a quick shower?"

"No prob, Bob. I'll make some coffee and just rifle through your things until you're ready."

I give a little chuckle and head toward my room. *Please, don't be serious. The last thing I need is the shower scene from Psycho in my life.* I close my door, behind me, and listen for a moment. The sound of the coffee pot being deftly dismantled provides enough reassurance that I grab an outfit and head to the bathroom. Even though I've seen nothing alarming in Noel's character (other than her quick adaptation into friendship), I lock myself in the bathroom and hop in the shower.

After a record shower time, I hop out, blow dry my hair, and get dressed. As I check my face and hair in the mirror, I think, *I really need to email Miles. I'm a terrible friend. When I get back,* I resolve, *As soon as I get home, I'll check my email and I'll let him know what's going on. Maybe even Skype him if he's not too busy.*

Of course he's not too busy! The chastising voice says, *You know very well that he doesn't have anyone to spend the holiday with and he probably won't even talk to you if you abandon him for too much longer.*

Ugh! These words of wisdom just make me feel worse.

Coming out of the bedroom, I see Noel, calmly sipping a cup of coffee and reading a book from the shelf. She smiles up at me, over the black rims, and says, "Ah, now you look like you've joined the land of the living!"

If only you knew! I think. Then, I realize she does know. I pretty much told her. *She must be nuts if she's still hangin' around. I wonder what she's after...* I smile back at her and say, "Just about. I need a cup of coffee before I go anywhere or see any more people, today."

"I put your cup, right there, next to the pot. I had a feeling you'd be wanting some. Now, while you drink your coffee, let's decide on where in the wide world we're going to go. You'll have to drive because my rocket ship is in the shop." She gives me a little wink and my inner-monologue runs rampant, *Yep, nutty as a bag of peanuts and just as harmless unless you get hit, full force, with it.*

Smiling and trying not to laugh, lest my laugh should be detected as being a little bit at her instead of what she said, I take a sip of my coffee, then say, "I like the breakfast idea. I could go for some hashbrowns and bacon."

"Potatoes and pigs it shall be. I know just the place. Whenever you're ready, Madame Navigator!" She gives a little giggle at her own silliness takes a drink of her coffee as she leans back into the chair.

17

Knowing that I can't eat very much, I tried to find something that had a little bit of everything that I wanted. It's a crappy problem to have but I know I could have worse problems relating to food. Noel seemed to have the same issue and couldn't decide on what she wanted. When the waitress came to take out orders, Noel told her that we were sisters and both had a hereditary medical condition that prevented us from being able to eat very much. Gesturing with a bony hand and wrist, she pointed at the back side of the menu and asked if the lady would allow us to order from the senior citizens side. Wide-eyed and in awe, I watched Noel's completely serious face as the waitress looked at us both with pity and said, "Sure thing, honey. You two tell me what you want and just don't let anybody know I did it, m'kay?"

We both ordered tiny sized meals and hot chocolate with whipped cream, eyeing each other slyly as the waitress left to place our orders.

Overall, it was an enjoyable evening and I was glad that she got me out of the house. I kept thinking about Miles and mentally kicked myself for not bringing my phone. I could have at least sent him a text or something. I learned more about Noel and her background but no more about why she had been in West Regional. When the waitress came with a refill of our hot chocolate, Noel pulled out three different pills, thanked the woman, and swallowed them in front of her. No doubt with the intention of keeping up the allusion that we're suffering from some illness. Based on what she did tell me and this clever trick, I could guess that her visits to the clinic were related to depression and anxiety issues. It was odd to hear sad or unhappy thoughts from someone that seemed so happy all the time but I know that even the happiest of people are usually nursing some sadness or other.

On the way back to my house, I decided that I would ask her if she stayed any longer but, as we were getting out of the car, she told me that she had to go because her parents would be back soon and she didn't want them to worry. We exchanged numbers and she told me that she'd check in with me tomorrow. I tried to let her know that I would be fine and that she really didn't have to worry about me. "Well," She said, "We never really know when we need another person until someone saves us or there's no one around and we fall." With that, she smiled but I thought I could catch a little sadness in her eyes. She turned and followed the path through the snow that she had formed, leading from my house back to hers.

~~~~

Inside my quiet, little house, I put another scoop of grounds in the filter, without emptying it, and filled the water tank about halfway. I wasn't going to make the same mistake of reheating coffee to a thousand degrees before trying to swallow it. I woke up my laptop and loaded my email. I knew Miles would get a kick out of hearing about Noel's stunt with the pills. Five emails from Miles are waiting for me to be read and the oldest one is from two days ago. That heavy feeling of being a crappy friend descends on me and I exhale a deep breath.

"Okay, let's see what you have to say." I click on the oldest message so that I don't miss anything in his stories. The subject line says 'Astral Projection' and I roll my eyes a little. Miles has been investigating a few aspects of our condition and likely thinks this phenomena holds some answers.

Several weeks ago, I had had a 'dream' about my friend's son being shot. In that dream, I yelled to try and get someone's attention but nobody heard me. There was one kid, however, that seemed to recognize that I was there and also seemed to recognize me later on. Miles had similar experiences but hadn't ever seen the same person later so he was intrigued. He had found one or two others like us, since he started looking, so he had also promised to report on whether or not they'd had similar experiences. Settling in to my chair, I begin reading his first message.

'Well, after little thinking and much whiskey, I've come to a few potential theories. One of which is astral projection but 'astral' doesn't exactly apply in our cases. Astral projection is represented in several cultures (including natives and Inuits) and denotes the ability of the soul or consciousness of special people to travel into other worlds.

Like heavens, hells, alternate universes, you name it. I never really gave it too much thought cuz it just didn't really fit but since it came to mind, I gave it some time.

Anyways, what I did find (that relates to us) is called 'etheric' projection. That would be the soul or consciousness of a person traveling in our current realm.

Well, I couldn't find to much solid info on it but it got me thinking. If tribes had Spirit Walkers, they could have actually just been people with the ability to project astrally or etherically. If our

```
consciousness were to enter
different areas of existence,
that brought me to the idea of
a mind's eye.  Could one
projector see another with the
"mind's eye"?  If they can,
could that explain how people
can feel like they know each
other without having ever met?
 Well, then on top of that,
does that mean that everybody
does it but only some people
know that they do?  Its a deep
and philosophical subject,
hence the much whiskey.  Lemme
know what you think.'
```

Before replying, I get up and fill my cup with new coffee and think over what his message said. Anybody with this kind of 'disorder' looks for answers and especially during their teenage years so astral projection wasn't new to me. For a good stretch of time, somewhere around fifteen or sixteen, I had just about convinced myself that it was, in fact, the answer. Now, etheric projection wasn't something I had stumbled upon as a kid and it was an interesting concept. I could see the black hole forming in my mind as I tried to wrap my head around some of the possibilities.

I sat down and sent Miles a lengthy reply; half apology, half thoughts on this new subject. It seems to me that there projection of the soul is what's going on but there's no scientific proof of it so it's hard to tell. Now, if we could get a bunch of us together, maybe we could start making some connections. One of the main points that I wanted to portray to Miles is that, without every one of us keeping diaries (and who knows how many there really are), we still can't even provide any evidence or proof, ourselves. The memory of the kid that seemed to recognize me comes back and I wonder, *If I could find that kid, would he know me? And, even if he did, would he admit it? How do I even know that kid was there? What if the whole thing never happened?*

No! I tell myself, *It did happen because you have a scar on your palm to prove it. I don't know who the kid is or if he could even be found. If he was found, there's no real, safe way to even talk to him without his parents calling the cops. Just drop it and move on.* I shake my head with some bitterness at the logic of this thought. I'm right and I know I'm right. I might not ever know. I add these last few thoughts to my email, more for my benefit than for Miles, and decide to go to bed. His other emails would just have to wait until tomorrow morning.

Full, worn out, and exhausted, I haul my blankets from the couch and climb into bed with my clothes still on. I feel the cold plastic of my cell phone against my hip so I pull it out of the bed and plug it into the charger on the night stand. I breathe a deep sigh and remember the meditation techniques. The quiet darkness is comforting for once and I can feel myself drifting. The weight of the blankets makes me absent-mindedly kick my feet out and my right foot hangs slightly over the edge of the bed.

Happy thoughts of Clark and the moving process to come should get pushed out of my head but I like them better than the mindless breathing. Imagining and half-dreaming about morning coffee in his kitchen, I'm completely relaxed and comfortable. The sound of a little kid, a giggle that is muted somehow by what may be water, makes me open my eyes and look into the darkness of my ceiling. I hear the carpet rustle and all of the hairs on my body stand at attention. *Why didn't I keep a light on? You idiot!* I hold perfectly still and listen, not even breathing. Something makes a cracking sound off to my right and my whole body twitches.

Debating whether or not I should get up and run or stay silent and wait, I feel a warm, wet thing quickly slide up my heel to the pad of my foot. A girly shriek escapes me as I yank my knees up to my chest and desperately rub the wetness off of my food. My stomach churns violently as I wrack my back against the headboard. Adrenaline hits my muscles and I bolt out of the bed and land on my knees, just feet from the door. Without a look back, I barrel straight through the unlatched bedroom door, knocking my hip against the frame, running as fast as I can to the front door. Fumbling with the locks, I wrench the door open and launch off of the stoop and into the snow. Now a safe enough distance from the house, I sit down in the snow and watch the house as my tears steam on my face in the darkness.

18

I sit in the snow until my mouth feels numb and my feet ache, just watching the house. Nothing moves inside and there are no sounds. I stand up, wavering a little from the cramps in my knees, and shivering with every part that isn't frozen. Cautiously, I move forward a little toward the house. A car horn, from some other street, makes me jump and my brain wakes up. *This is ridiculous,* I think, *There's nothing in there. There's no way anything could have gotten in there. Just suck it up and go back inside before you freeze to death!*

Heeding these words and trying to dissolve my body within itself, I shamefully move toward the open door and the darkness beyond. *Why didn't I turn a light on, on my way out?* Reaching the doorway, I pause in front of the house and peer inside.

"Anyone there?" I call out. A snide inner-voice answers me, *Yeah, 'cause they're just going to tell you they're hiding under the bed.* Reaching inside with my left hand, I feel around for the porch and entryway lights. Finding them, I flip them both up and recoil a step as the shadow of a person disappears in front of the dining table, across the room. *It's just your eyes playing tricks on you. Go in the house!*

But I don't want to go in the house! I answer back.

Okay, then Clark can find a human popsicle in front of your open door when he picks you up for dinner tomorrow. Do what you want.

An exasperated sigh struggles through my chattering lips and I take a step into the entryway. *I wish I'd left my scratchy blanket on the couch instead of taking it in my room. Man, I'm an idiot...* I take another two steps into the house and grab the handle of the door without looking at it. Still listening and hearing nothing, I prepare myself to check behind the front door. *Okay, we're gonna do this on three. We're gonna pull it forward just enough to glance behind it and then put the eyes back on the room. Any creepy bastards hangin' out behind the door are gonna get hit with it and we'll back out the way we came.*

Okay, sounds good. Let's do this. I reply to myself. I let the air out of my lungs in a slow breath, still keeping my eyes on the room in front of me, and grip the doorknob a little tighter. A co-mingling of inner-voices chants, *One, two, THREE,* and I rip the door toward me and look into the empty crevasse of the corner. I point my eyes back to the living room and slowly close the door behind me but let it rest just on the latch, without closing it.

Staring into my house, I'm conscious of the burning feeling in my feet and I'm pretty sure that they're actually melting, at this point. I want to look down at them but my eyes are still riveted on the door to my bedroom and the hallway opposite. A full minute passes and just stand there, waiting.

There is nothing there! Will you just get on with it, already? The thought makes me realize that I've been holding my breath as I listen so I try to focus on breathing. A giggle reaches my ears and I realize it's coming from me. Placing my hand on my forehead, I can feel fresh tears tingling in my eyes and I begin to laugh uncontrollably. *That's it, that's the ticket,* the snide voice continues. *Just laugh like a crazy person and anyone in here will feel like they're the ones that are trapped.*

Laughing even more at this new thought, I start to double over. Tears are forming and beginning to roll down my cheeks but not from fear. "It's okay!" I say to the house. "You can come out now. Haha! I've completely lost it so you can come and take me! Mission accomplished, assholes!"

The warmth of the house is starting to calm my shivering so I stand there, waiting for my laughing to subside. I take a few deep breaths and resolve to start turning some lights on. Slowly, and pausing in every doorway to listen, I walk through the house and flip them all on, randomly giggling as I go. Nothing and no one greets me so I grab a blanket off of my bed, unplug the phone from the rarely used charger, and head out to the couch. A check of the time on my phone tells me that it's a little after 2am.

With incoherent and unfinished thoughts, I debate sending Noel a text message but decide to do it anyway. My brain doesn't want to think in a straight line so I simply text, 'Sorry for the hour, having a tough night. Wondering if you were up.' I sit on the couch, just staring at the phone, for over four minutes. No beeps or responses come and my eyes begin to burn.

I realize that I am incredibly tired but I don't want to go to sleep. Not here and not yet, at least. I raise my eyes to look at George, my new Aloe Vera plant, and try to focus on thoughts of Clark. Reminiscing about a time that we took a walk, I find myself smiling at the comforting memory of his arm around me. I let my eyes close for a split-second longer than a blink and it feels so good. His smile and his laugh make me feel a little more like I'm a part of reality. I give myself another blink, just slightly longer. My tired eyes burn in that good way, like they're letting you know that they need a break from work.

Opening them again, they've gotten watery so I try to wipe the liquid away, one at a time. Lowering my hands onto the pile of blanket in my lap, I close them again for a short respite. I relax a little as an image of Noel's pretty eyes and her laugh comes back to me. Slowly, I begin to open my eyes but fling them wide as I realize that there is a face, distorted by moving shadows, right in front of mine. I inhale sharply and try to jump backwards, away from it, but there's nowhere for me to go. The shadow person disappears and I feel anger building up inside me as I call out, "Will you please just leave me alone?!!"

"That's it." I say to myself. "I'm not just going to sit here." I pick up my phone, grab my keys and wallet off of the kitchen counter, slip on some shoes, and head out to the car. Once inside, I realize that I don't know where I'm going to go. *Should I just drive around? Find a place for coffee?* Without even thinking it, the resolution sets itself that I'll just go to Clark's. *Besides, he gave me a key.*

I pull carefully out of my driveway and start down the road. *What are you going to do when you get there? Say, 'Sorry, Clark, I had a bad dream'? What if he's not home?*

Then, we can let ourselves in.

Right, and get arrested or shot when he finds us. Brilliant.

"Okay," I say out loud. "I'll just see if there are lights on and we'll go from there."

As I turn the corner on Clark's street, I can pick out his house by his truck parked at the sidewalk. I can't see the front windows yet so I'm not sure if he might be awake. *You should have called him, first. How's it going to look if you call him now?*

Another voice replies to the thought, *Like a stalker, that's how.*

I roll my eyes at my own ridiculousness and slow down as I get closer. I can see now that there are lights on and flashing blue and green colors from a tv. A little part of me lights up with joy but comes crashing back down as I recognize that there is a car in his driveway. At 2am on Christmas Eve, there shouldn't be a car in his driveway unless it's mine.

Go knock on the door, see what he has to say! If he's got some other girl in there, that's kind of important info!

Send him a text and ask him what he's doing!

No, I can't do that. At two in the morning, I will actually BECOME a stalker if I do that.

Instead, I just drive back home without really paying attention. So many thoughts and possibilities flood my mind that I almost miss my own driveway. Backing up on the icy road, tires slipping just slightly, I put the car back into drive and pull up to my house. I turn the car off and just sit in the quiet until all the heat has been replaced with the chilly night.

Heading into the house, I check my phone again and see no messages or phone calls. No additional footprints in the snow tell me that Noel hasn't stopped by. Feeling defeated, lonely, and now confused, I go inside and sit back down on the couch. Looking at my plant, I ask, "What do you think, George? Who was at his house?"

George seems to respond telepathically by simply pointing my eyes to the bottle of vodka and Bloody Mary mix that was intended for sharing my tradition with Clark.

"Great idea, George. Do you take ice?"

19

A knocking at the door makes me irritatingly aware of the pounding in my head. *Please just go away*, I think to myself. Another short series of knocks forces me to sit up on the couch and I hear a little voice come from the other side.

"Hey Jo, it's me, Noel. Are you home?"

"Yeah, just give me a minute." I say, as I look around the living room. The Bloody Mary bottle is a quarter full and laying on its side and the vodka bottle has just under half of its original contents. Getting up, I say, "I think it's open. You can come in as long as you don't judge."

A little laugh accompanies the turning of the handle and daylight momentarily blinds me. She takes a few steps in, looks around, and then gives me an empathetic look. "Oh you poor thing, you had to drink alone?"

"Well, George was here and I think he counts."

Puzzled, she looks at me with a slight tilt of her head and says, "Who's George?"

Feeling silly now, I point to the Aloe Vera on the coffee table. "Noel, George. George, meet Noel."

With a quick laugh, she leans toward the coffee table, "Nice to meet you, George. I see you were good company." She reaches out and grabs the bottles off of the table, slipping one finger into the lip of my used glass, and heads toward the kitchen. I hear the refrigerator open and close and then the familiar chink of a glass bottle being placed in the freezer. She turns the faucet on and I can hear her filling my cup to soak.

Normally, I wouldn't let a guest take care of anything in my house but, today is not a normal day. "Thank you." I say, rising off the couch.

"Hey, no prob, Bob. What are friends for? Why don't you sit back down, before you fall over, and I'll make some coffee."

A surprised laugh accidentally escapes my lips and I drop back down, and not very gracefully, onto the couch. The movement causes my brain to slam into the side of my skull and I immediately regret it. "Aughhhh," I let out a little moan.

Noel laughs at me and then goes about the business of making coffee. While she's occupied, I take a few minutes to look her over. Her hair is curled and done up, makeup on a paler than usual face, but she's wearing a large black t-shirt, maybe three or four sizes too big. Blue jean cut-off shorts and winter boots. A little confused, I look back up at her face and see that her usually cheery mouth is pursed in the corners. Not wanting to offend her but wanting to know what's wrong, I settle on the least invasive question I can think of, "So, how did your day go? What time is it, anyway?"

"Well, not too great actually and it's around three, I think." She looks at me and gives me a little smile but I notice that her eyes aren't sparkling and they're a little red.

"Are you okay? Do you want to talk about it?"

She sighs heavily and pours the water into the pot. She turns it on and comes, silently, to sit on the couch. She opens her mouth, as if she's going to speak, sort of staring but not looking at the room in front of her. She fidgets and turns on the seat and starts again, "Well, we went to my step-mom's family for an early Christmas dinner. It was going pretty good for a while but my dad wouldn't really talk to me. Not this morning, in the car, or even when we got there. He was just... weird. Well, then..." Her voice cracks and I see her eyes film over with water and I instinctively reach my hand out to comfort her. She jumps back, away from me, and her eyes get wide. She half-whispers, "Not yet."

Oh, dear lord, I think, *What is wrong with this girl?* "I'm so sorry." Lame but it was all I could think to say.

"Oh, no, you're fine! I'm the one that's sorry, bringing my drama when I know this isn't the drama club." She laughs that light, airy, easy laugh so I smile.

"I should make this a drama club. Lord knows I've got enough of it to qualify. If you don't want to tell me, that's fine, but what happened at dinner?"

She takes a deep breath and exhales through partially closed lips and looks back at the ground. "So, someone that was sort of new to the family asked me how my mom died. I don't know who, just some guy that was dating or married to someone's kid. I told them a little about what I've told you." She pauses and looks at me, as if checking to make sure I remember what she had said before.

"Anyway, when I was telling the guy, I had a funny feeling and thought that maybe I had remembered that it wasn't my dad that pulled me down the stairs. I thought that maybe it was the firefighter that got me out of the house. I was wrong, of course. I'm not exactly, you know, a reliable source." She chuckles and points the index finger of her right hand at her head and twirls it.

"You're not nuts!" *Or, maybe you are, but either way...* "There's nothing wrong with getting confused or mixed up. I'm sure that was a tremendously difficult night for everybody."

"You're so sweet! So, anyway, I say the thing about the firefighter and my step-mom says to everybody, 'She doesn't know what she's talking about! It was Dave' (that's my dad) 'that pulled her down the stairs.' Then, my dad, still not looking at me, grumbles," In a voice that I assume is meant to mimic her father, Noel says, "'She's on some new meds.'"

"What a jerk! I'm sorry, I shouldn't have said that about your dad."

"No, it's okay. He kinda is a jerk. So, then, when we were done with dinner and people were clearing plates and getting the pies and stuff, my dad gets up from the table, knocks his vodka over, onto my lap, and, when he tried to… I don't know, reach for me, steady himself, stop the glass from falling off the table… He pulled the tablecloth and the candles fell over." She motions down at her clothes and says, "The tablecloth caught on fire and one of the candles landed in my lap and caught my dress. It was a really nice dress."

I can't help but just stare at her in disbelief. *How could she not be thinking what I'm thinking right now? Does she even think like a normal person?* Another voice pops up, *She's not a normal person and that's why she doesn't think that. Besides, you weren't there and she's a grown adult. If she believes it was an accident then it probably was.*

Noel gets up from the couch and fills two coffee cups with the new pot. "It was okay, just a little scary. But then, when we got home, he made me take the new medicine, even though I'd already taken some. I loved that dress." She hands me a cup of coffee. "Anyway, I can only stay for a little bit. They're taking a nap and he said I have to be in before lights out."

"Thank you." I say for the coffee. "Um, what kind of medicine are they giving you?"

"I don't know. They won't give it to me. It's like a powder and they put it in my drinks."

"No offense, Noel but that really doesn't sound like... Well, it doesn't really sound normal. Have you had that kind before?"

"Nope, I don't think so. I think this is the first time. I'm not sure. I don't like it, though, it makes me want to throw up. Actually, I better go. I don't want to get in trouble and I'm not feeling very good. Here, you can have my coffee for when you're done." She gently places the cup on the coffee table and gets up.

"Are you sure you have to go? You haven't been here for very long."

"Yeah, I'm sure, but I'll see you again. Maybe tomorrow." Pausing at the door, she does her best Terminator impression (which, for a newly 30ish young woman is not great), "I'll be back!" I laugh as she exits and closes the door behind her.

20

I could hear Noel trudge through the snow, as she headed toward her parents' place, and I thought more about the things she had said. *Maybe they're capsules and her dad opens them up to make sure she actually takes them. All the same, I wish I knew what she was being medicated for and what with. Something still just doesn't seem right there. Besides, who am I to judge? Her dad and step-mom have known her way longer than I have and they probably have to deal with stuff that I know nothing about.*

This realization made me feel much better about the situation so I chugged my cooling coffee and grabbed Noel's mug. *Time to give Miles some attention*, I think, as I head over to my computer. Even though my head hurts and I don't want to stare at tiny black letters on an overly-bright screen, I need to. It's Christmas and people like us need to stick together. I also have some phone calls that I need to make. *Yeah, like asking Clark who the heck was at his house last night...*

Nope, later, we'll deal with that later. Now is the time to be a good friend to Miles since we've been so bad, lately. Settling in the chair and waking up my machine, I reach over for the pot and refill the cup. My email comes up and I see that there are no new replies from Miles. *He's probably waiting to see if we just dropped out on him.* I find the oldest, unread message, right above the Astral Projection subject. This one is titled Native Americans and Prophets. Clicking on it, I read:

> 'Well, doing a little more digging into the book you saw, I found some interesting stuff about Native Americans. This doesn't relate to spirit walkers per se but it does have some interesting stuff. I probably knew this already but I found that alot of tribes had prophets. These prophets were relied on to speak to the Earth, animals, and spirits and bring the information to their tribe. Some of it seems kind of silly like asking certain animal spirits to bring them game or plants for harvest but some of it could relate. Well, anyway, I read that some of these prophets could tell when people were going to die and could know if certain 'souls'

were at rest or not.   There's
still not a ton of info on
these kinds of people because
nowadays they're considered
mythological or just stories.
 One of the things in how it
relates to what I've read about
Spirit Walkers is that alot of
tribes believed the prophets
could walk in the physical
world, the world(s) of the
dead, and even the worlds of
the great spirits.   They could
do a lot of things that we
can't so I'm wondering if we
start documenting what happens
in our dreams and find more
people like us and try to
communicate more during the
dreams (scary thought, I know),
maybe we could find more
answers.   Well I know it's not
the most practical of thoughts
but it's where I'm at right
now.   I'll let you know when I
find more.'

With constant thumping, my brain reminds
me that it is still inside my head, as I try to form
some coherent remarks. I get up to grab some
Tylenol and feel psychosomatically better even
though my inner-voices are still a little muddled
and slow. I intend to type out a brief reply but end
up writing nearly an entire page on my thoughts on

prophets. I've had experiences, in the past, where I would clearly see things, short dreams that didn't make a lot of sense, at the time, but then those things would come to pass. I've also had an uncanny ability to know what number someone is struggling to recall or is thinking of. Not your usual 'pick a number between one and ten' kind of thing but rather, 'what's 10,382 times 47 and divided by 6' kind of thing.

Now, the number thing, I tell Miles in my email, can easily be written off as a fluke that just occurs on a random basis but the Presque Vue experiences, of dreaming something that hasn't happened yet, is an odd phenomena that could fit with the prophet details. I know that people generally say, 'Yeah, right, whatever, you made that up', but, when these dreams happen and I recognize them, I find somebody, anybody that might be around in a few years, to tell about it so that I can say, 'write this down or remember it and then I'll prove it to you when it really happens'. I know that Miles won't judge or try to break down these occurrences by saying that I make them happen. I know that I can trust him to understand that I couldn't possibly describe the inside of a house in which I've never been or detail a conversation with a person that I haven't even met yet. He'll get it and, I actually hope, he'll have them, too.

After detailing some of these experiences, in my email, the thought strikes me and I add it for

Miles. 'If we could find more people like us, we might actually be able to prove that some of this stuff happens. Start our own research into how we are the way that we are and find answers for ourselves. After all, it seems that people like us are the only ones seriously interested in what MAKES us the way that we are.' Giving a deep sigh, I decide that I've written enough on that email and add the line, 'Merry Christmas'. I hit send and reach for my coffee cup. Distractedly, I attempt to take a big chug but end up spilling it all over my shirt because it has gone completely cold.

"Ugh!" I say to myself, out loud, wiping the wet lines in the sad attempt to dry my shirt. I wipe my, now wet, hand on my pants and press the button to return to my inbox before getting up and putting my full cup in the microwave.

Standing and watching the timer as it slowly ticks down from 30 seconds, I find myself reliving the experiences of driving by Clark's house. The itch to call him and try to find out what was going on almost takes over and I turn to look at my phone on the counter behind me. There's a light flashing that denotes either a missed call, a message, or a low-battery. I haven't quite figured out what color of light means what, yet, so I pick it up and swipe its face.

A text message from Clark surprises me and I feel an apprehension at reading it. The voices in my head take off, competing with one another to see who's going to be heard first. *He's breaking up*

*with you. He met somebody else. — No, he's going
to ask where you want to have dinner. — He's
saying he changed his mind about living together. —
Someone broke into his house last night and
watched movies on his television until dawn. — He
joined the military and he's shipping off to another
country and won't ever be able to see you, again.*

I make a little growling sound at these inane
thoughts and just tap the icon to see what he
ACTUALLY said.

Sent: Today at 1:37pm	Dixon, Clark says…
	Hey beautiful! Merry Xmas! How about your place tonight for steaks? My mom dropped by and is going to be staying with me so if you'd rather have dinner with just you and me let me know. If you're okay with entertaining someone else2 then we'll do it at my place.

Something in my stomach does a
somersault and there's a slight feeling of a firework
going off behind my sternum. *Well,* I think, *That
answers that question.* I send him a simple reply:
'Can't wait to see you. Up to you, your place or
mine. You choose.'

21

Clark and I settled on dinner at my place with dessert at his. His mother was planning on leaving the next morning so he figured it was as good of a time as any for us to meet face to face. She was a very pleasant woman, early sixties, she had grey hair and that tired librarian or retired school teacher look. Clark had driven to my house and then took the both of us to his, after dinner. On the way, he explained that his mother's house had a tree limb fall on it, due to being over-weighted by snow and age, and the roof was being repaired. "Why she didn't call me before it fell is beyond me but I'll be going over to take care of the other branches, after the house is fixed up." He had said.

Giddy at the news that this was not some old flame or recent harlot (and probably owing partially to the wine consumed at dinner), I was more than happy to meet his mother with open arms; even though she was a hugger and I'm not.

Clara, as she protested the formal Mrs. Dixon, served dessert; a crème brûlée that she had just 'whipped up'. She had apologized for dropping in and taking up so much of his time when we 'must certainly would have wished to be alone together'. She seemed so sweet and caring and like she actually knew me that it was easy to fall into the motions of having known her prior to that night.

She kept the embarrassing stories of Clark to a minimum but promised a lunch date, when her house was repaired to give me the real dirt and pictures, to boot. After dessert wine and then Champaign for us ladies (because Clark had to drive me home), we hugged goodbye and made plans for a lunch, later in the week. Clark told her that he'd be home after a bit. With mock conspiracy, Clara had winked at Clark and said, "I won't wait up!" They both laughed merrily at the blush that had overtaken my face.

Extremely wary of what might happen, given my recent rash of 'episodes', I had told Clark that I didn't know if it was a great idea for him to stay the night. I really, desperately wanted him to stay, to be my protector, but I didn't want something awful to happen and have him decide that he didn't want to deal with my personal form of drama in his own living quarters. He assured me that he would be there for me, through thick and thin, happy and sad, 'hurling fists or ice cream'. Knowing I was being selfish, I told him that he could stay.

The remainder of the evening ended up being the most passionate between us in our relationship to date and I slept like a baby. For the first time, in a long time, I had a happy dream and not your run-of-the-mill nightmare. I woke up to the feeling of him kissing me on the forehead, early light coming through the edges of my window shade, and him saying goodbye. Happy, warm, and safe, I fell back into a dreamless sleep.

~~~~

Slowly, I become aware that I am now conscious and awake. The familiar feeling of my blanket and my bed let me know where I am and I don't even have to open my eyes. Brief snippets of the night before begin replaying in my mind and I roll over to place my arm on Clark. As my hand touches empty bed-space, I open my eyes and see that he isn't there. Confused, I sit up and look around the room. *Where'd he go?* I'd been taught long ago that, whenever I can't find something, the first step is to start with the last place that I remember seeing it.

Sitting up slightly, in the bed, I hold the sheet to my bare clavicle and think. *Let's see, dinner here then dessert there, a cup of coffee for him and a beer for me on the couch, we went to bed...* I take a quick look under the sheet and discover that that was apparently accurate. *Okay, so... Kitchen? Bathroom? Where did he go?* I reach toward the end of the bed and grab some clothes.

Slipping them on, I listen but hear nothing but stillness from my house. I get out of bed and check the bathroom but it's empty. Heading to the kitchen, I find a note on the table:

'Dearest Johanna,
 I kissed you goodbye before I had to leave but wanted to thank you for the great night. It was the best Christmas yet. Hope you have a good day today and I'm looking forward to seeing you again. I need to get home and make sure mom's house gets fixed properly. You never know if you can trust guys to do it right for an old lady. ☺
 XOXO,
Clark'

The feeling, that I can only assume precludes dancing and shouting from rooftops, overcomes me and I smile like an idiot as I re-read the note. I stop myself before I smell the very paper for any trace of his scent that he may have left. Placing the paper back on the table, I turn to the coffee pot and open the filter container to make a pot but find fresh grounds in it. I lift the lid of the water tank and see that, it to, is full and ready. *Awe...* My inner-voice gushes, *What a sweet man!* Liquid starts to form in my eyes and blurs my vision so I close the lid and push the start button.

Hastily grabbing my phone off of the counter, I type a quick message to tell him how sweet and thoughtful he is and how much I enjoyed spending time with him and meeting his mother. Doing a silly, little dance, I put the phone back on the counter, swaying and humming, and head toward the bedroom to take a shower. I grab clean clothes from the dresser and burst into a head-bobbing solo, singing, "What is love? Baby don't hurt me, don't hurt me, no more!"

Once I make it into the bathroom, my singing dies out as a memory of an uncomfortable bath-time experience overtakes my memory. I shake my head to dispel the distasteful memory and turn the water on. Probing the reaches of my memory, I find another song to try and focus on. With an unsteady voice and a lot of 'hmm, hmm, hmms', I settle on the much easier, "Once, there was this kid, who, got into an accident and couldn't go to school..." Singing throughout my shower, I emerge from the tub, belting out, as loud as I can, "Now clever feet that flicker that fire, and burn like candles in smoky spires, do more to turn my joy to sadness than somber thoughts of burning planets, shut the—"

My phone ringing, in the kitchen, stops my mouth from producing the next words to the song and my body freezes in what Madonna would call a 'Vogue". Wet, dripping, and in my towel, I run to the kitchen with a smile on my face, expecting it to be Clark.

22

Picking up the phone and sliding my finger to the right, I say, "Hello?" Silence greets me, in return. "Hello?" I say again. I hear someone take a deep inhale with a faintly feminine intonation. "Noel? Is that you?" I pull the phone away from ear and look at the number it registered. *Yeah, that's her number.* "Noel, are you there?"

A little cough follows and I hear her voice, quiet but clear, "Yeah, it's me. Are you busy?"

"Yeah, no, I'm not busy. What's up? Is everything okay?" I say, looking down at the small puddle forming on the floor.

"I wanted to let you know that I won't be able to come by later. I'm pretty sick, today. I think it was something I ate... Or maybe something's eating me. I'm not sure which but, whatever it is, I think a tapeworm would be more pleasant at this point." Noel inhales sharply and says, "Oh gosh! You don't think I have a tapeworm, do you?"

I laugh in spite of her seriousness and say, "Well, now, that depends. What are your symptoms?"

"Oh, you know, vomiting from orifices that shouldn't be vomiting... The occasional loss of all muscle control... I'm not certain but, either there were little green men in my bedroom or I might be hallucinating. What do you think, doc? Am I gonna make it?"

Throughout her description, I can't help but giggle and I try to stifle an open mouthed laugh. Composing myself, I say, "Well, it sounds like a nasty case of food poisoning. Do you have any medicine? And fluids, you're supposed to have fluids. Are your parents there?"

"No, they left early this morning. My step-mom woke me up and gave me my medicinal beverage and then I heard the car pull out of the driveway. That's all I can remember because I fell asleep again. Well, that is until the volcanic god in my stomach decided it was time to sound the alarm. I've been like this for at least a few hours. Or maybe days. I don't know. Time seems irrelevant at this point."

"Oh, you poor thing!"

"Do me a favor, will you?"

"Sure! Absolutely! You want me to sacrifice a virgin to appease the volcano god? Though, to be honest, Noel, I don't know that I know where to find a virgin at the moment."

She laughs but cuts off quickly with a groan, "Please don't make me laugh... I don't think pressure in my guts is a good idea, right now."

"Sorry!"

"S'Okay. Um, since you have a car, can you maybe bring me something that might make this better? Or, at least bearable? I don't have any cash but I can try and find some in the house."

"Don't worry about it. I'll find the closest virgin drugstore that I can and be there in a jiff. Just try and relax. What's your house number?"

"2212. Just come on in; I'm pretty sure that the door is unlocked. Just call out when you come inside. If you don't hear any response, just back away slowly, and call a HAZMAT team. And DON'T let them bury me in that red dress. I hate that dress."

~~~~

Parking in front of 2212, I look out the window at Noel's bluish-grey townhouse. It's the same style as mine but two floors, wood panels at diagonal angles, heavy curtains blocking the view through the windows, and a large, brass knocker on the brown front door. Even though the yard is covered in snow, I can see that it's well taken care of. Thorny rose bushes line the exterior of the lawn, chopped heads point like spears, deterring visitors. I grab the shopping bag from the seat next to me and turn off the engine. *Keys, phone, money, medicine.* This mantra of remembrance prompts another thought, *When was the last time that I took MY medicine? I don't even know where it is...* I make a mental note to find it, and take it, when I get home.

Heading up the walk, I peer, slyly, at the neighbors houses, waiting for some watchful neighbor to ask what I think I'm doing in someone else's yard. With no one in sight or a twinge of a curtain to denote a watcher, I approach the front door. Avoiding the heavy knocker, I have the faint thought of not wanting to leave fingerprint evidence that I've been there. Instead, I ball my fist and rap my knuckles twice on the door. I had intended to knock three times before opening the door but the cold, hard wood threatened to split my skin open.

One more, quick, sideways glance, and I reach for the handle. *Right, because innocent people that have been invited, look to see if someone's watching. What a dummy...* I take a quick breath and open the door. "Noel? I'm here!" I call out. A smell of cinnamon and something else greets me as I step into an immaculate living room. White carpet covers the floor from wall to wall and polished, no doubt expensive, furniture sits on display and, for a second, I wonder if I've just stepped into a model house. Fake flowers adorn the coffee table and plastic fruit sits in a bowl on the dining table, across the room.

"Noel?"

"I'm upstairs! I'm in the bathroom. Just give me a minute. Come on up. My room is the first door on the right! ...No!!! The first door on the left! Do NOT come in the first door on the right if you value your life!"

I chuckle and take one more, quick glance around the room and step onto the carpet from the entry. Realizing that the fruit and flowers are not actually fake, I back up immediately and remove my shoes. "Okay, I'm coming up!" I call out. I double check the carpet to make sure that I didn't get it dirty and head toward the stairs. I polished wooden rail lines the sides. White carpet is covered with a rug that runs down the middle of the stairs. I can't help but wonder, *What would people in third-world countries think if they knew that Americans covered wooden stairs with carpet and then covered that carpet with a rug?* Another inner-voice replies with authority, *Yep, this is why they hate us.*

Reaching the top of the stairs, I look to my left and to my right, not remembering which door led to death and which to safety. "Noel, was it left or right?"

From my right, I hear, "The left. First door on your left is my room. Just go in there and I'll be out in a minute." A flushing sound finishes her sentence and I chuckle a little under my breath. *Poor girl...* I hear the sound of the faucet running so I head to the left and go inside the room.

The sight of pink walls immediately makes my eyes roll. A white, border wall-paper shows a corseted lady, enjoying a beach scene with her parasail in mural style. A white, four-poster bed with a pale yellow comforter sits, disheveled against the wall on my left and a matching bookcase overflows with stuffed animals and books. On my right, I spy a white window-seat with a padded, fringed, pillow so I head over and sit down.

The door swings inward and I see a very pale and slightly greenish Noel enter. "Hi," she says. "Are you here to bury me?"

23

Even though I had told Noel to call if she needed anything, I didn't hear from her for the rest of the night. I spent the majority of the evening chatting with Miles via Skype in between the occasional text from Clark. Miles had been trying to find more people like us and he was doing some research into how difficult it would be to set up a forum and just what it might take to ensure people were properly vetted before being allowed access. Clark was detailing the projects that were going on at his mother's in between texts about how excited he was that I would be living with him.

The evening had passed and was fairly uneventful. Sometime around 11, I realized that I had forgotten to eat but didn't feel hungry. I forced myself to eat a piece of bread while I learned more about how forums work. I had found that it was surprisingly easy so Miles and I decided that we would do it. He set it up and made me an admin so we started our new project.

A little after midnight, we decided that we had a good beginning and that we'd pick it up again tomorrow afternoon. Miles was trying some new techniques for sleeping so he had to sign off. Alone and on my own, again, I decided I'd try to read a book until I felt tired enough to possibly sleep. I grabbed one from the shelf that I'd been meaning to read and curled up on the couch.

~~~~

A voice, from somewhere in the kitchen, says, "I'm ready." It startles me so much that I jump in my seat and my book falls to the floor. Sitting perfectly still and not picking up my book, I listen while simultaneously replaying the voice in my head. It was a man, pretty old, and not one that I recognize. A thump and a crash, from the voice's previous location, sends me hurtling over the arm of the couch and I smack into the frame of my front door.

I steady myself and listen more intently than ever. My breath is stopped in my lungs and I hold perfectly still as I look around the room without moving my eyes, lest even that simple movement could make a noise. Silence answers me. Feeling a little silly, I take timid steps around the couch and try to look into the kitchen. I don't see anyone or anything that could have made the noises or the crash.

Now positive that this is all in my head, I relax a little and allow myself to breath. I adventure farther across the living room and stop at the dining table. Placing my hand on the wooden back of one of the chairs, I lean slightly forward and look around the island counter that holds my coffee pot.

A very loud -GARRRRRR!- makes me jump straight up, into the air, and I stumble backwards, falling over my own feet, and crashing down onto the floor. I crab-walk backwards, as fast as my limbs will move me. Four feet back into the living room, I turn and crawl, on all fours, back to the couch. Climbing and clawing, I get back up on the couch and cover my head with my blanket. *Oh shit, oh shit, oh shit!* I think. My breathing comes in labored, pulsing gasps and I know that, if I don't calm down, I'll hyperventilate.

Under my shroud of blanket protection, I try to force myself into Lamaze breathing while the hairs on my arms tickle as they stand up. A ringing begins in my ears and my stomach threatens to unload its contents. No more sounds can be heard and I quietly whisper, "Please, please, please go away. Please be gone!" I get my breathing down to a normal rate but the ringing continues and my heart feels like it's going to explode.

Still hearing nothing from the world outside of my personal fort, seconds feel like minutes and minutes feel like hours. I finally decide that it must be safe enough to pull the blanket down. Slowly shifting my arms to grab the front of the blanket, I grip a little of the fabric and stop to listen. Still hearing nothing and only seeing what uninterrupted light that my covering would allow, I pull slightly until I feel the edge of the blanket resting on the top of my head. Stopping again, I listen and my heart rate begins to slow. Nothing crosses the light in front of my vision.

I reach my hands up a little higher and allow my fingers to enter the forbidden zone, outside of the blanket. I grip the edge of the blanket and hold it over the top of my head and wait for some otherworldly creature to bite my fingers off as a slithering feeling crawls up my spine. With no new events, I take a deep but quiet breath and begin to slide the covering down over my face.

As soon as my eyes are uncovered, I find that I'm staring straight into the face of an old man in a black suit, white shirt, and black tie. His mouth is agape, most of his teeth are missing, eye sockets just black holes, spidery black veins twine up his neck, and he has bright white hair atop his head. I shriek with a volume that I didn't even know I had and jump backwards and toward the door again, falling, head-first over the edge of the couch.

Coming down with a crash, I continue shrieking, loudly. The voice of a very sad old woman, on the verge of tears, says, "Jimmie?" from somewhere in the room and I slam my already injured head into the wall. My vision goes black and sparks erupt like a firework in my brain. The woman's voice comes again, angry this time, and says, "Evil, wretched girl!" I put my hands out in a pathetic attempt at defense since I can't see anything or anyone until the burning in my brain subsides.

The darkness that clouded my vision and my thoughts subside and I blink a few times to make sure that my eyes do still work. Looking desperately from side to side, I realize that the man is gone but that everything has changed. Instead of the living room with the couch in front of me, I'm in a darkened bedroom, facing an unmade bed. A dresser is to my right and a lit doorway is just further passed it. Breathing fast and quick, I jerk my head from side to side and try to remember how I got here. *Am I even here? What if I didn't wake up? What if I'm not dreaming? What if I'm in Hell?* "Oh jesus!" I say in a whisper.

Security of simply 'being' starts to return as nothing comes for me and there are no noises save my labored breath. Slowly, I start to raise myself up by sliding my back up the wall behind me. Looking around the room again, I realize that I am in my own room and not the living room. I place my hand over my thumping heart and try to slow my breathing as my tears begin to fall, stinging my eyes.

"Why is this happening to me?!"

24

I move my computer and power cord to the couch and sit in the full wattage of every bulb in my house. I couldn't sleep now, even if I wanted to, so I resign myself to wasting away the minutes until dawn by Googling whatever random thing comes to mind. After several, unsuccessful attempts to drown out the voices in my head or distract them by fun websites, I look at the clock on my phone.

2:43am

That gives me 17 minutes to go to the gas station and buy some sleeping pills or beer, I tell myself. A mere five seconds is wasted during my rumination so I flip my computer onto it's top, set it on the cushion, grab my keys and wallet, and head out the door.

Not having given any thought, whatsoever, to the effect of slippers on an icy driveway, my right foot slides out forward too quickly, my back foot begins to follow the momentum, and my right receives lift to execute a full cabaret kick. The speed of which brings my left foot off of the ground; leaving me with nothing but an uncomfortable cushion of air until my backside lands with a cracking sound and my head offers the crescendo. I had a hair clip, pinning my hair up, and my only hope is that the cracking sound of my skull was really just the plastic hairclip hitting ice-covered concrete.

I lay motionless and listen for the sound of laughter that I know will come but I hear nothing. Slowly and painfully, I gain a seated position; still too embarrassed to touch my head, even though I know that it is very dark. *Well, there goes two minutes, dummy, get up!* Still not admitting injury, I raise myself a little higher and get onto my knees. Picking up my items from the driveway, I pretend that I'm looking for something under the car. To give the dramatic piece a believable effect, I reach under the car for an imagined object. *The laughing and pointing will start any second now...*

I give my searching hand another full two seconds before I pause, mid-reach, as if I've found my goal. I retract my arm, head burning and spinning, and pull myself up to standing with the smoothest motion possible. Once on both feet, I dart my eyes around the neighborhood, without turning my head, and unlock the car. Nothing but the wind moves down my quiet street so I get into the car and start the engine. I still don't want to peruse my obviously damaged scalp with my fingers until I'm safely away from any potential onlookers so I put the car in reverse and back out of the driveway.

I keep my head straight forward, as I drive down my street, and try to keep my eyes on the snowy road. I slow a little as I come upon 2212 and I gaze up at the house. A light, on the second floor, flicks off and my brain tells me, *It's because she saw you and your Special Olympics back there and has to hide her embarrassment, of even knowing you, in the darkness.*

As soon as the house is safely in my rear-view, I allow my hand to raise up to my injured head. Locating my hair clip, I squeeze to release the pressure on my hair and put it in my lap. I'm pretty sure it's broken but not positive just how bad. Returning my fingers to my scalp, I gently finger the area that would have taken the blow. It hurts, a lot, and I finally understand the definition of 'it smarts'. I force myself to touch the rising lump, one more time, and withdraw my hand to my lap. I try to see my fingertips but can't as there are very few streetlights. I'm pretty sure that my fingers are wet but not positive if it's blood or snow. I resolve to keep my right hand in my lap until I reach the gas station and can examine it more clearly.

Turning the next corner, I see the station in front of me and my brain registers 'gas station'. The voice of the reincarnated schoolmarm in me says, *Fueling station! Even propane is a liquid, here.*

The only gas you can buy is a hot dog and nachos! It's a liquid station.

The thought of liquid returns me to my debate of sleeping pills or alcohol. Sleeping pills don't always work for me but alcohol seems to be doing the job. Neither is good for me and both are addictive. Sleeping pills are cheaper but also easier to overdose on, *Easier on which to overdose*, I add, for the little old biddy, in my head. I can wake up, if I don't take enough pills and they're not guaranteed to work. On the other hand, if my house catches on fire, with alcohol, I'm likely to die, snoring away. An image of Noel's melted skin flashes through my mind and I shudder.

Hastily, I pull into the station and turn off the engine while the car is still in drive. I move the shifting rod to park and roll my eyes at myself. I pull the keys from the ignition, with one hand, and careful touch the back of my head, with the other. Still feeling a wetness, I open the car door and examine my fingertips under the light. A little smear of blood, but not too much, pronounces the creases of my fingerprints. *It's fine*, I tell myself.

As I get out of the car and head in through the doors, I check the phone again: 2:52am. With a minimal amount of time to decide, my brain continues the debate so I head toward the drug section. *Sleeping pills don't always work but alcohol seems to. What if you get a call about the job tomorrow?*

The snide voice chimes in to answer, *Yeah, and what if you don't wake up to answer it?*

The trusted voice of reason and logic speaks up to this challenge, *We have that potential detriment in both cases, it's true. However, we can limit the effect of alcohol by limiting its consumption. The same cannot be said for pills. There is a likelihood that pills won't work, causing more to be consumed. The way I see it, it's a 50/50 cost versus benefit in both cases with one caveat. That caveat being that you've already consumed a good deal of alcohol in the last several days. Do you really want to continue this trend?*

With a nod, that I hope the cashier didn't see, I begin to browse through the available drugs. Everything from tampons to Tylenol meets my eye but no sleeping pills. A quick check of the phone shows that it's 2:56am. I'm running out of time since they stop selling at three.

I quickly (but not too quickly) head to the beer area and grab a 12 pack of Corona. Hefting my load to the counter, I set it down, pull my ID out of my wallet, and poise my debit card to strike.

The cashier scans my case and smiles as he looks at my ID. "Just barely made it." He says, handing me back my ID. "Beer run for a late night party?"

Thinking back over the visions of the old man and my complete lack of understanding my own personal time-line and the voices in my head, I say, "Yeah, a VERY late night party and I wish they would all go home!"

He winks at me and instructs me on what buttons to push, after I slide my card. "Well," he says, "Just hope you can get rid of 'em by New Years because people will be wanting alcohol then, too."

I finish pressing buttons and decline the receipt with a simple, "No thank you but thank you." I grab my beer from the counter and head toward the doorway, secretly wishing that I could be rid of them by New Years. The only problem, that I can see, is that they're obviously not here for the beer.

25

Before I even opened up one of the beers, I took the precaution of drinking two, full glasses of water and two pain relievers. Not trusting the other residents of my house to let me watch a movie or read a book in peace, I took my beer to the spare room and worked on packing up the boxes. At first, I was very analytical and careful about what to keep and what to toss, separating things into piles, and taping completed boxes. But, after three beers had been finished, the packing and sorting went much faster. The to-go pile ended up becoming a full sized garbage bag and the to-keep pile was placed in whatever box was handy. When the last beer had been opened and my stomach told me I'd had enough, I clumsily picked myself up off of the floor and wobbled down the hall toward my bedroom.

~~~~

Opening my eyes, I realize that I'm awake. Brief snatches of the dream I was having are still present in my mind. The more I try to hold onto them and analyze them, the faster they dissipate. The only clear image remaining is that of a playground with a brightly colored plastic structure, complete with a slide.

I try to roll over, onto my side, and go back to sleep but my brain has been activated and won't let me so I just lay there, enjoying the comfort of my pillow and blankets. Nothing important is happening today or tomorrow, or even the day after that. No reason to get up. The next big thing on my calendar is a New Year's Eve party with Clark and that's not until Sunday. *Maybe I could sleep until Sunday...*

Maybe you have slept until Sunday. Do you know what day it is?

This last thought makes me open my eyes and really put some effort into thinking. *Let's see, Christmas Eve was Sunday (breakfast/dinner with Noel), so Christmas was Monday (that's when I had dinner with Clark), um... yeah, yesterday was Tuesday and Noel is sick. That makes this Wednesday.* I roll again, in the bed, onto my back and stare up at the ceiling. *I should probably get up and check on her. After all, she would have been here by now if I were the one that was ill.*

With a slight moan, I sit up in the bed. *After coffee. I need coffee if you expect me to function.* I move over to the side of the bed and look down before placing my feet in the territory belonging to the under-the-bed monsters. Seeing none (as they're usually nocturnal), I slip my feet into my slippers and make an attempt to stand. Wobbling, stiff, and sore, I sway on my feet and my knees begin to buckle as I fall back onto the bed. My brain sloshes a little with the sudden movement but otherwise I feel fine. *Must have slept in one position for too long.*

Instead of trying again, immediately, I stretch my arms and back. It feels phenomenal. I look around my room, as I prepare myself for another attempt at standing, and see that there's quite a bit of yellow daylight coming from the living room. A yellow sky will be a nice change compared to the grey overcast that we've had lately so I find a little more motivation to get the coffee going and I head into the living room.

Once the coffee pot is gurgling away with its daily duties, flashing 12:00 at me, I wake up my computer to see what time it is. I make some mental plans to drink coffee, check emails, get dressed, enjoy the sun, and visit Noel. The light from the living room window invigorates me and I can't help but smile as I open my inbox. Since it's only, actually, just after 1:30, there is a lot that I can get done today.

My email reports that I have four emails from Miles, two special offers to enhance my libido, one holiday sale for a business that I've only purchased from once, and a message from

Facebook to point out that I don't visit often enough and I might want to check in and see what's new. *Lame*, says a voice in my head. *Maybe your phone is more popular.*

"Yeah right!" I reply sarcastically.

Marking to the two messages as spam and deleting the other, I try to find other reasons to put off reading the ones from Miles. Without opening the spam folder, I click the nifty little button to delete its contents and stare at the unread messages from Miles. Miles is a great guy, smart, funny, and like me, but I don't really feel up to engaging in our treasure hunt for information just yet. Being an introvert, there is a certain amount of human interaction that I can take before my alone time needs refilled and I feel like I've maxed out and am on empty. Even though it's just a few emails, it still requires a certain kind of thought. For introverts, or those with social anxiety, a simple text conversation can be draining and tedious. The desire to find the correct words and be perfectly understood can make it difficult to want to engage in any conversation at all.

Knowing that Miles is probably used to delays in my responses lately and that he would completely understand if I bothered to tell him, I decide to get up and check out my phone, instead. *Maybe when the coffee's done,* I think, *Then I'll actually read one and reply.*

Picking up my phone from the counter, I swipe the screen and see that I have two missed calls and five voicemails. For the average person, this would be disconcerting to have the number of messages exceed the number of calls but I completely understand it. Since no one of importance would actually leave me a message (and nor would anyone that knows me), my phone has been accumulating messages over the last month. I check the call log and see that both numbers are unknown; one local and one out of state.

With a sigh and an eyeroll, I hit the button to listen to the messages. As soon as it connects, I put it on speaker and turn to wash the accumulating glasses and mugs on my counter. The unfriendly, robotic female voice tells me in odd pauses, "You have- five- new- messages and- one- saved- messages. First new message- sent- Friday- December- 15th—"

Static ensues and I furrow my brow, turning to look at the phone over my shoulder. I can hear people, in the background of the static and then a man's voice starts to speak so I turn back to the stained coffee mug in my hand, "Hello, my name is Ken and I'm calling because you recently submitted your information to win a special bridal party from 'It's You!'." *Um,* my inner-voice interrupts, *No, I sure didn't.* "I'd like to confirm the details with you and get your address so that we can ship you this very exclusive wedding party package, prior to your special day. This no-cost to you gift will contain a coupon for a free Bride's t-shirt, invitation samples,

party gifts for your bridesmaids, and lots, lots more. To claim this awesome deal..."
"That's quite enough of that, thank you very much." I say, wiping one hand on a towel. I push the 7 button on the dial-pad and delete the message. The next message begins and it's a wrong number. The same person calling for the same person that doesn't have this number anymore and has been told repeatedly that Katherine doesn't live here. Having recognized the voice, I push the seven and delete the message. The next message is a hang up so that one gets deleted before I turn back to my dishes.

"Hi, this message is for Johanna Parks. This is Thomas Croft from E&M. So, listen, I'm sorry to leave this on your voicemail but I'm actually at the airport, about to board a plane and I'll be very busy for the next two weeks and I'm not sure when we'd get a chance to chat. I just got news that the corporate is cutting the position that you applied for and the new store has hold up's so we won't be able to bring you on but we do hope that things will get smoothed out, in the future. If that happens, we'd like to keep your info on file and contact you to re-interview, if you're still available when/if that happens. Anyway, I gotta get on this plane. I sent you an email so just feel free to reply and let us know if we can hold your data. Thanks and sorry again for the voicemail."

Drying my hands as quickly as possible, I try to hit the number 4 to replay the message but my still wet fingertip smudges the screen and hits the seven. "Ah, crap!" I say to the phone as the robotic voice announces that the message has been deleted and begins the next one. Another spam message plays and I delete it with perfect dexterity. "Seriously?!" I ask the phone. With a little bit of anger, I pound a bit too hard on the end call button and my phone mocks me by changing the screen to my text message inbox and continues talking to me.

Taking a breath to steady myself, I gently tap the buttons and return to the active call and end it. I wipe my hands on a dishtowel, again, and go back to my computer. I hit the refresh button on my inbox but nothing comes up. I furrow my brow and realize that the email from the Irishman at E&M could have gone to the spam folder. I click on the link for the world's most unwanted emails and it smiles back at me with cruelty; 'Hooray, no spam here!'

'Cause you emptied it, you dummy!

26

Feeling completely crushed and now hating the outside world, I'm forced to think about what to do. I had told my landlord that I would call as soon as I'd heard back about the job. This was NOT the outcome I wanted to be giving. I'd also have to tell Clark that I would be broke because all of my money from my temp jobs would be needed to pay for the next month's rent. *Hopefully he'll be okay with a poor person moving in next month.*

I pick up the phone and find my landlord's number. Sighing, I rub my forehead with my free hand and try to decide just what to say. Instead of calling, I select the text message option and begin typing, 'Hi. Just found out that the job for which I had applied was temporarily canceled due to corporate issues. I have almost enough to cover the rent for January so I can give you what I have if you can work with me and get the rest when I get some more money. I apologize for the delay and the issues. Please let me know how you would like to proceed. Thanks'. I hit the send button and put the phone on the counter.

Turning back to the sink, I turn the hot water on and begin to wash another mug. Putting some fresh soap on the sponge, I try to rub the stains out of the cup and my phone rings from behind me. Dropping my hands into the sink and releasing all control of the muscles in my neck, I drop my chin to my chest. *What now?!* I place the mug in the sink, rinse my hands and wipe them on my pants. "I'm coming, I'm coming..." I say to the phone.

Picking it up, the caller ID tells me that it's my landlord. With another sigh, I swipe the screen to answer it. "Hi Jerry." I say with as much optimism that my throat will allow me to drum up.

"Hi Jo, got your text. Here's the deal: I've got someone that wants your place and wants it now and they'll pay more since the market's gone back up. How soon can you get out?"

"Uh, um..." My landlord has always been direct and to the point but I figured two and a half years of living here would garner me just a little bit of softness.

"Hey look, I'm not trying to be insensitive or anything but I've got to tell these people whether or not they can have it or they're going to move on another place. Sorry about your situation."

"Oh, no, I can totally understand. I just wasn't expecting that. I didn't know you had people lined up."

"What business did you think I was in, sweetheart?"

I cringe at the use of a such a familiar term and realize that, since day one, he was not saying it to be cute or amiable but was actually kind of condescending. "Well, how much time can I get?"

"I'll make you a deal. You be out by the 1st and I won't charge you anything, even for carpet cleaning. So long as you leave the house in good condition and do some decent cleaning, I can even almost guarantee that you'll get your deposit back. I've seen the way you live and trust that there haven't been any wild parties or anything." I can almost hear him implying that I'm a loser and have no friends.

The thought of being able to keep what money that I've saved and going to live with Clark with the hope that I'll have a sizeable deposit coming to me, I tell him, "Okay, let me make some calls. I'll send you a text and let you know for sure, one way or the other."

"Cool-cool. Get it done. Again, sorry about your situation, honey, but this is the way of the world."

"Right." I say and hang up on him. *What an ass. How did I not see it before?*

Because people are always nice and sweet when you're going to give them money. Duh. You weren't born yesterday.

I can feel tears starting to prickle at my eyes and I let out a ragged sigh. *Now, I need to call Clark and tell him that I can't keep my place and hope to god that he'll let me move in. He's probably not even ready for me.* I sniff and find that my nose is running. Desperately trying to keep the tears from falling, I locate a tissue from inside my bedroom, and sit on my bed to blow my nose.

Waiting a few more minutes until I'm sure that I can speak without my voice cracking, I go back to the kitchen and pick up my phone. I try out my voice, before I dial, to ensure that I can sound happy and like somebody that someone would want to live with, "Hi Clark, it's Jo." *Good enough*, my brain says. *Let's get this over with.*

I found Clark's number in my list of recently contacted numbers and press the call button. As soon as it starts to ring, I feel a wave of sadness come over me and I'm not sure that I can have the conversation. I contemplate just hanging up and trying later but the ringing stops and I hear Clark's voice from the other end, "Hey beautiful, I was just thinking about you and wondering what you were doing for dinner."

I smile and feel my chest involuntarily heave with the threat of sobs and I swallow so hard it makes my throat hurt. "Hi Clark. Funny you should mention what I'm doing for dinner. I'll be packing."

"Finally gonna take the plunge and try out my house for a bit?"

What does he mean 'for a bit'? Ignoring the thought, I smile again, hoping that it might alter my voice just enough so that he won't know how I feel. I begin to trace lines on the kitchen counter with my fingertip and unsteadily continue, "So, yeah, I am. I just got off the phone with my landlord and he's offering me a really good deal. He says that, if I move out by Monday, he'll do what he can to let me keep all of my deposit because he's got another person lined up for the space. And I—" my voice breaks and I can't finish the sentence.

Caring and compassion is in his voice as he gently says, "You what, babe?"

"Well, I also got a call for that job I was trying to get and they had to cancel the position so it looks like I'll be broke, moving, and jobless all at the same time." I can't help but laugh out loud at my own situation and a voice in my head rolls its eyes and says, *Good going! Why don't we just go over every reason why he should just run away, as fast as possible, in the other direction.*

"It's okay. Keep your chin up. Let me finish up on this job and I'll come get you. We'll find somewhere and have a nice dinner and then get to packin' yer stuff. Don't worry about it. Besides, sounds like your landlord is kinda a jerk. You figure out what you want for dinner and we'll go there." After a brief pause, I hear him give a little chuckle and he mockingly says, "My treat."

27

Clark picked me up and took me to a Mongolian restaurant for dinner that night. Afterward, we had planned to pack some of my stuff but the offer and temptation to stay at his place was too much so nothing got done at my house. The next few days was crammed with packing, cleaning, and moving. I didn't think it would take long to move what little I had to his house but I forgot about the reality of moving. One house didn't need two couches, two beds, two coffee pots, et cetera. We ended up keeping his couch, my bed, and his coffee pot. I couldn't bear to part with mine so it went in a box, in the garage.

Working at a break-neck pace, we got everything moved and cleaned by the middle of Saturday night. I slept during the days and Clark went with me during the evening. At night, he'd go home and I'd stay up until dawn, cleaning or doing whatever I could think of to avoid sleeping in the dark. I met the landlord, on Sunday morning, to hand over my keys and do a walk-through. He was very happy with the state of the house and kept his condescending comments to a minimum when I explained that I would be moving in with my boyfriend. I was happy that Clark wasn't there because we hadn't even discussed if there was a title for our relationship, yet, but Jerry didn't need to know that.

With plans to go out that night, I felt rushed to get out of the old house and into the new one. I had to locate an outfit and unpack some of my things so that I could be ready to go. Jerry was polite and quick and even wrote me a check for my deposit (minus the cost to rekey the locks, of course) right there, on the spot. I thanked him and, with one last look, thought about all of the memories that had occurred in that space. How scary it had become seemed silly now that it was empty and filled with light.

Noel had stayed away because she was afraid that she might get me sick with the plague. I had only visited her one more time and that was to bring her some medicine and apple juice. I couldn't fathom why her parents wouldn't be providing medicine since she was so obviously sick but I didn't want to meddle. I told her to call or text at any time and we made an agreement to go out for a breakfast dinner on Wednesday or Thursday, hoping she would be better by then. I looked at her house as I drove by, on my way to my new, shared abode, and didn't see any signs of life from the house. I was sad to be moving away from her but, in reality, it wouldn't be that far for me to drive and, at some point, she would have a car again. I felt positive that we would stay friends in the years to come.

~~~~

     After a very casual dinner of Chinese take-out, Clark and I decided that it was time to get ready for the party. The New Year's Eve party was being hosted by his brother, Clarence, and his partner, Andrew. I hadn't been to a party in a very long time but was very much looking forward to it.

     "Have you seen a box with makeup in it?" I ask Clark.

     "Umm... No, I don't think so. Was there other stuff in it?"

     "Yeah, like my shampoo and stuff like that. It would have been one of the last boxes to come over. It was mainly makeup and nail polish. Stuff like that."

     He thinks for a moment and shrugs his shoulders with a shake of his head, "No, can't say as I have. What was written on the box? I'll check the garage."

     Reddening slightly, I look him straight in the eyes and admit, "Jo's war paint."

     The red in my face increases as he explodes with laughter and a little sliver of saliva comes out of his mouth. This makes me start laughing and, wiping his chin, he laughs so hard that he closes his eyes and I see a water forming in the creases. I get control of my laughter and say, "But, seriously, I need it. I've got to take a shower and wash my hair. I'm covered in the carnage of murdered dust bunnies and am just gross."

Continuing his laughter, he turns and heads out the front door, toward the garage. I hear him mutter something but can't make it. Replaying his reaction in my head causes me to laugh even more at myself. I try to stifle it because I know that laughing at oneself is supposed to be a sign of mental weakness. A giggle escapes, every now and then, as I look through each box in the dead animal adorned living room, again, and I try, repeatedly, to clear my throat in hopes of stopping the fit.

Once I'm confident that every box has been checked and rechecked, I follow Clark's path out the front door and to the door that leads into the garage. I find him, serious and methodical, checking names of boxes, opening them up and closing them, and placing them in a stack, behind him. Enjoying this first time experience, I watch and absorb the details; hoping to cement them in my memory. His muscles flexing as he lifts a new box onto his work bench, the way he silently mouths the titles written in Sharpie, how he looks with some expectation at the contents, and then the disinterested change that comes over his face as he closes them back up and places them in the stack.

After two boxes and him not noticing me, I realize I had better say something and stop wasting time. "Anything yet?"

He jumps, slightly, and I know without knowing that this will be the first of many times that my ninja skills of silent entry will scare him. I see a slightly red flush flash over his face and he smiles at me, then says, "Nope, nothing yet. Are there still boxes in your car?"

My right hand raises and I stop it before a full-on, face-palm can initiate. Sheepishly, I raise my hand to my head and scratch my temple, giving him my best 'sorry-for-being-an-idiot' look, "Yeah, actually and that's probably where it is."

"Ha! That's okay. I'll run out and check. Is it locked?"

"Oh, I can do it. You've done enough recon for one night."

"Well, not trying to rush you or anything but I don't like to be late and we need to get a move on if we're going to be there in time. I'll go check and you hop in the shower. If I find it, I'll bring it and, if I don't, you can use mine."

I widen my eyes and raise my eyebrows as I think, *You have no idea how girl hair works, do you. I can't just use yours.. I'll look like a homeless person and not your hot new live-in lady-friend person. And, bring it to me? In the shower? While I'm naked? Do you know nothing about me and my incredible OCD regarding modesty?*

As if he could read my mind, Clark raises his own eyebrows and says, "Okay, or you could look or I could knock two times, set the bottles outside the bathroom, and let you know when I've cleared the area... Either way, babe, we've got to get moving."

"Okay, you look, I'll shower. Three knocks and drop the package just inside the door. And, I feel I should warn you, if I need to be somewhere at a certain time, Mother Fate will do her damndest to keep it from happening. Make sure you've got fuel in the truck, your wallet in your pocket, keys to your house, brake lines in full operating order, and road flares, just in case."

Before he can speak another word, I give him a wink and spin around, walking back toward the front door of the house.

28

On the way to Clarence and Andrew's, Clark seemed to appreciate my situation. Completely wet hair in the end of December is not a good thing and, since he didn't own a hair dryer and I couldn't find mine, Clark turned the heater of his green F350 up full-blast. We drove to the next town over with the windows down, sweating our buns off but our teeth chattering, in the redneck version of a 70 mile per hour blow dryer. With hair like mine, 'wind-blown' is not an issue, it's a style. And, besides, I couldn't really care less what people thought of my hair, so long as it's clean and I know that it won't frighten small children.

I couldn't ask any of the questions that I was dying to know, due to the onslaught of wind from both windows, so the ride was done in silence. After several twists and turns, I was starting to think that, either he was lost, or we weren't really going to a party. One more right turn into a nice looking neighborhood with big houses, Clark rolled up both windows from the panel on his armrest. Slowing to a respectable 25, he looked over at me and said, "Hope it's dry 'cause we're here."

I pulled the visor down and took a look in the illuminated mirror. *Could be better but it could be a hell of a lot worse.* I make an attempt to run my fingers through my unruly mane and pull my legs from a cross-legged position, off of the seat, to place them in my black, high-heeled, open-sandaled style shoes. My calves have to flex to even put them on and I silently hope that there won't be a lot of standing or walking during this visit. Another look in the mirror tells me that my organic lip-gloss will need to be applied during the duration of the evening and that no amount of makeup is going to hide the scar, mildly hidden in the crevice between my right eye and the bridge of my nose. *Let's just hope no one wants to compare scars...*

~~~~

A long line of cars, on the block, let's me know that we have arrived and Clark pulls up behind one. I have no idea to which house we're headed because the vehicles extend as far as I can see, down the road. *Oh great, lots of people.* I re-apply some lip gloss as Clark cuts the engine. "Wait here," he says. I wonder what I'm supposed to be waiting for and, subconsciously, turn to the back seat to see if there is something, some gift, that I didn't notice before.

Coming around to my side, he opens my door and offers his arm to support me as I attempt to exit the lifted beast on unsteady legs. Trying to gingerly grab his arm for my descent, he smiles and says, "You look really beautiful, tonight. Did I tell you that?"

Surprised by this compliment from nowhere, I stumble a little, as I step down onto the snowy sidewalk. Doing my best to recover, I look down at my black, form fitting, spaghetti strap shirt and well-fitting size 4 jeans and say, "No, I don't think you did but I have a bad memory. What did you say?"

He laughs and says, with a little more gusto, "I already know that you're going to be the sexiest lady here. And, you'll be with me so that's even better."

I can't stop the laugh that comes out of my mouth. *Tonight is going to be awesome!* I can't think of anything to say in retort so I push my phone and wallet down into my back pockets before he locks the doors. I know that having a phone and wallet, sticking out of the pockets of my pants is on the list of no-go's for being sexy but, since I don't carry a purse, I don't have a lot of options. Also, since I don't have a key to his truck (...*yet*), I can't exactly leave them if I need to make a hasty retreat. *Besides,* I remind myself, *I'm here with Clark. I should be perfectly safe and not need to leave, without him.*

"So," I say, "I've met your mom. Who else will be here that I might need to memorize? Your dad, siblings, other cousins, crazy old aunt, stuff like that."

"Well, there is my mom but my dad and his wife are also supposed to show up. His name is..." He stops and turns toward me so I stop walking. The weight of our bodies causes the snow below us to compact and make crunching noises. "Okay, I'm going to tell you this but you have to promise not to laugh or make fun of him when you meet him. You have to promise."

An honestly-confused look moves my eyebrows up and I genuinely ask, "Why would I make fun of him?"

Clark gives a tired sigh as I see memories flash across his eyes. "Because," he says, "His name is Christopher Robin Dixon."

"Um, okay..."

I see his eyes light up with a subdued hope and he gives me a mildly quizzical look. "Christopher Robin."

"Yeah? I don't get it."

He laughs and his easy-going nature returns as he about-faces on the sidewalk, toward the party. "Christopher Robin is the kid that had Whinnie The Pooh. I figured, you of all people would get that."

No shame or embarrassment at missing the connection can stifle my "Oh yeah! I remember! I LOVE Whinnie the Pooh." And then, the slap of the first mental facepalm of the night forces my mouth shut and I wait for the impending onslaught of teasing. Clark continues walking and doesn't say anything so I add, "Was it on purpose? Naming him like the character, I mean."

He takes my arm in his and gives a little chuckle before planting a kiss on my forehead and I feel like a little kid that just got the inside joke. Pausing before we cross the street to a very well-lit two story, he looks down at me and says, "No, it wasn't on purpose. We have a family tradition to reuse some names and it just worked out that way."

"My family has the same tradition," I say, as we make our way across the street. "That's so funny. I'd love to learn where your tradition started because I'm very interested in that aspect of anthropology. On my dad's side, everyone gets a variation of Joe (thus the Johanna) and, on my mom's, we have two middle names that come from family. For example, Johanna comes from a person on my mom's side but is also a variation of Joe so that seems like sort of a no-brainer and then my middle names are—"

The front door flies open so quickly that both Clark and I jump a little. An extremely tall, fit, and drunk-looking black man, in a black, silk shirt, greets us with a huge gleaming white smile. He comes forward, through the doorway, and grabs Clark's biceps with both hands, pulling him forward in a hug. "Oh my goodness! You're here!" he exclaims in a slightly high pitch. His shoulder-length, straight, black hair reflects the porch light.

Startled, I back up a half step and watch the exchange. The drunk man releases his hug into a casual hold of Clark's shoulders and says, in a rather feminine tone, "I heard you were coming but I just didn't believe it!" He lets go of Clark's shoulders and claps his hand in a prayer position, in front of his chest. "Oh my goodness! I'm just so happy! And, JEALOUS!" He quickly eyes me up and down, two or three times. Swiveling his head like a bobble-doll, he returns his eyes to face Clark, with an even bigger smile, "Who is this sex-ay young thang? You devil, you! She's absolutely GORGEOUS!"

Clark turns beet red in the yellow light from the porch and I don't even try to hold back my smile or my enjoyment at his obvious discomfort. He clears his throat and says, "Andrew, this is my girlfriend Johanna, Johanna, this is my brother's partner, Andrew."

With a smile bordering on laughter at this impromptu meeting, I offer Andrew my hand and he grips it softly and sweetly as I say, "It's very nice to meet you, Andrew."

Andrew slips his arm around my shoulder and, looking directly at Clark says, "We need to get this young hotness something to drink and she's going to dish me all the dirt on what you've been up to lately!"

"You two do that." Clark says, and laughs, as I watch him over my shoulder, eyes wide with a mix of concern and excitement over this new adventure. He winks at me and asks Andrew, "Where's my brother?"

"Oh, Clare? Probably somewhere around the carbs. Check the table toward the patio where all the evil has been laid out." Looking to me, arm still guiding me through the white walled hallway and into a living room with three different colored walls and a mural of an old, grey-tree painted on the fourth, he says, "Now, tell me the dirt, honey, and I'll make all your dreams come true."

Looking around at the twenty or so people, talking and laughing, I can tell the party is in full swing and everybody is having a good time so I relax a little. Doing my best impression of the German, from Hogan's Heroes, I say, "I know nuss-ing!"

Guiding me to a table filled with various bottles of alcohol and juices, he picks up a plastic pitcher, filled with a red liquid and ice cubes, from the table and releases his hold of my shoulder to grab an open jar of green olives. Wiggling the pitcher and the olives in the air, he nods his head at me and says, also in a mock German accent, "Oh, you vil talk, ve have vays of making you talk. And, I hear that ze ways has to do vith... Oh, vut do you call zem.." Andrew turns his head to the side and closes his eyes, as if seriously contemplating this question.

Completely drawn into his little skit, I think *Wow, this guy is weird*. Fiercely and dramatically, Andrew opens his eyes wide and I jump a little. Without breaking character for a moment, he looks at me and says, "BLOODY MARIES! Oh, yes, little girl, ve know you're secret. Our double agent has told us all about it! Zo, vut do you say? One oh-lives for info and two oh-lives, for za secrets..."

A little giggle escapes as I try to mimic his complete seriousness. I look, slowly, to my left and then to my right, before leaning forward. I look up into his eyes and dramatically whisper with a subtle and quick raise of my head, "Make it five and ve have a deal."

29

Enjoying my freshly poured bloody mary and my olives, I listen to Andrew as he tells me how he and Clarence had met. We cross through the crowded living room and head toward a large marble fireplace where Andrew had left his drink on the mantle amidst a spattering of small, framed photos. Even though there were a lot of people in this space, with more coming in through the front door, the bodies parted like a sea in Andrew's wake. While he talks, I examine his face and I can't help but feel a little jealous and insecure. Without close scrutiny, one would think he was in his early thirties but I can tell it's more like mid-forties. His perfect complexion shines, in all the right places, with a softness that actually makes me want to be more girly.

I've never really known a man, up close, anyway, (or even a woman, for that matter) that has made me feel like I've done myself some sort of disservice by not being more glamorous. As he tells a gushing story about how he and Andrew had met several times but didn't ever really speak until they had literally been bumped into one another, my brain begins to wander and I think, *He's like the girlfriend that every girl wants but hates to have. Smart, pretty, funny, and way better taste than the average girl could come up with. Like that trophy girlfriend that you want to have come to all of your parties because you know that people will automatically respect them like they're a movie star and people will say, 'oh, wow, she's so awesome' just so that you can casually be like, 'yeah, she's my friend'.*

The voice of logic and reason answers my thoughts, *Don't kid yourself, honey. That man is far too glamorous to want to be friends with you. He's just being nice since you're dating his brother-in-law.* As if the wind in my sails cut out for a second, my self-esteem drops just a little bit and I know that the voice is right. If I was awesome enough to have a friend like Andrew, I'd already have friends like Andrew.

Snapping his fingers like a smelling salt below my nose, Andrew is looking at me with his head slightly ducked to try and see into my eyes. A little startled, I look up, into his face and try to smile as I feel a blush creep over my face. "What happened, honey? Did I bore you into a coma?"

"Oh, no! No, I'm sorry! I was just thinking and got distracted." *Distracted by thinking...*, the snide voice chimes in. *Good one. He won't think you're weird now.* Desperately, I try to recover but only make it worse, "I'm sorry. I mean I was listening and then I started thinking about you and that made me think of other stuff and I got lost. I mean, lost in my head... Oh jesus..." A sigh of defeat escapes and I smack my forehead with my palm. Laughing at myself while Andrew gives me his own curious but good-natured laugh, I say, "I give up. I'll just stop talking now. It's been a long day."

He places his hand on my shoulder and says, "It's okay, sweetie! Clark told us about the move and how you had to do it super fast. You don't worry about a thing. Tonight's your night to relax and let your hair hang out." Eyeing my slightly disheveled 'do', his face changes to a mixed look of slightly mortified pity and he says, "Well, you got that part down, already, so let's focus on the relaxing. Come with me." He places a large hand, gently, on my arm. "Let's go find Clarence. You need to meet Clarence. He'll love you!"

Doing as I'm bid, I turn with Andrew and we make our way, through the crowd, to a sliding glass, patio door. A plump and pot-bellied, bearded and bespectacled older man that could easily pass for a professor, is chatting with a much younger, clean cut twenty-something with the air of a self-important nerd, reaches over and pulls the door open for Andrew and I to exit.

"Thank you, Roger, darling!" Andrew says to the man and we both walk out onto the patio.

There are about half the number of people, out here, than there are in the house, and my claustrophobia and social anxiety calms a little. As we step under the line of lit, hanging lanterns, I turn to close the door behind us but, with a wink, the bearded man slides it shut so I mouth 'thank you' and turn back to the crowd.

Leading me around a small cluster of party-goers, greedily absorbing the warmth of the gas powered heaters, I see that there is a medium-sized fire pit in the yard and the majority of people are gathered around it; drinking, talking, laughing. As we get nearer to the group, Andrew bellows dramatically, "Where's my man?!"

People turn and laugh, pointing lit cigarettes off toward the right of the fire. "Excellent! Is everybody having fun here? Are you all being good little boys and girls?" A cheer rises up from the gathering and I smile at the easy abandonment so many people seem to have in social situations.

We make our way around and I look over all the faces, trying to pick out which one must be Clarence. A guy in jeans and a flannel jacket with a short, dark beard stands up from his leaning position against a large, landscape rock, and I see a little resemblance to Clark. Andrew quickens his pace and comes up next to Clark's brother, placing one large hand on the man's shoulder. Pointing at me with his martini, Andrew says, "Clarence, this is

Clark's young lady, Johanna. Johanna, this is Clare."

I extend my free hand as I step closer and Clarence takes it. With strength but gentle pressure, he gives it a shake and says, "Well, I've heard a lot of good things about you, Jo. Is it okay if I call you Jo?"

"Oh, yes, of course, that's fine. It's nice to meet you."

"Is Andrew being nice and taking care of you? Not being too catty is he?"

Andrew gives a little 'pshaw' and says, "Of course I'm taking care of her. Your no good brother off and left her, practically standing on the front porch!"

I open my mouth to protest this blatantly incorrect statement and then remember my manners. Instead, I say, "Yes, Andrew has been very nice. He even got me extra olives for my drink." As I say it, I realize that I still don't actually know how they knew I liked bloody mary's because I couldn't recall a time when I would have told Clark about it. With a slight chill and a shiver in my spine, I think, *What if Noel was their undercover agent and she's been reporting back about everything I say or do?*

"Excellent," Clarence says. "Clark said he was pretty sure you had ordered one once on a date but couldn't really remember. We whipped them up from scratch, just for you, so I hope you do actually like it."

With mock tempestuousness, Andrew gives Clarence an evil eye and says, "Who's this we you speak of? The way I remember it, I 'whipped' it up while your ass sat on the couch, watching football."

An inappropriate and improperly timed laugh bursts out of my mouth and I fling my hand over it as fast as my brain could get the message to it. "Sorry!"

Andrew eyes me with a little surprise and laughs at me. Clarence points at me with his index finger, holding a beer bottle, and says, "I like her. She can smell your bullshit."

My eyes go wide and I look up into Andrew's face, not daring to laugh. The corner of his mouth goes up in a half-smile and he replies with complete seriousness, "Oh no, honey, she's not laughing at me. She's laughing at your hideous beard."

A man's voice, behind me, says, "It is hideous, bro, you need a shave." An arm slips around my waist and I jump, preparing to smack whoever thinks they can claim ownership to my body.

30

As I spin and move away from the arm, I see that it's Clark and I exhale with relief. "Oh, it's you! You scared me."

Clarence retorts, "He scares me, too, honey. I wouldn't want him touching me, either."

Andrew shrugs and says into his martini, "I wouldn't mind."

Everybody laughs and Clark puts his hand on my lower back, kissing me on the forehead, "Sorry I was away so long. I ran into my cousin, Wendy."

Andrew asks, "Oh, where is Wendy? I wanted to talk to her."

"She's coming. She was just grabbing another beer and said she'd come out and have a cigarette."

"Speak of the devil!" Clarence says, looking over mine and Clark's shoulders. Instinctively, I turn my head and see a tall, thin woman with straight, natural blonde hair. She smiles at everybody with a wave and a sip of her beer and I know that I've seen her before, somewhere.

My brain kicks into overdrive, trying to locate her place in my memory before she gets any closer and I may have to admit that I can't remember who she is. *Wendy, Wendy, Wendy... Gah!* Coming closer, she sticks her beer bottle under one arm and pulls a pack of cigarettes out of her coat pocket. Sliding one out, she holds it between her fingers and puts the pack back.

"Hey, Clare, Andrew!" Her voice shoots like a thunderbolt through the haze of my memories and brings forward an image of her and our friend, Macy, from back when we were in college. In my memory, we were bowling in the student building and she was telling us a funny story about a really bad date that she had just gone on.

"I know you!" I blurt out. "How are you?!"

"Oh my god! Jo! Heyyy!" She opens her arms wide and we hug.

To my right, I hear Clark ask, "You know my cousin, Wendy?"

Smiling and with our arms gently wrapped around each other's waist, we turn back to the group. I release my hold of her and slip my arm through Clark's. "Yeah, Wendy and I went to school together. We had a few of the same classes. I know we're in a pretty small zip code and all but what are the odds?" I back at Wendy and say, "Why didn't you tell me your cousin was so hot?"

"I did tell you! I also told you that he was single and that you should meet him. Remember when I was going to camp at the lake for the whole of spring break and I invited you but you were too much of a scaredy cat to go? You asked what he did for a living and I told you he was jobless and broke. You said no thanks!"

Completely overcome by embarrassment at this statement and with my mouth half open, I look at Clark. He crosses his arms over his chest and gives me a smug smile. "Really. You said that, huh?"

"Um, I..." Looking to Clarence and finding that he, too, is now crossing his arms over his chest and giving me the same amused and smug disapproval, I look to Andrew.

"Don't look at me, honey. I'da said no thanks to broke and jobless, too, but you're on your own with these two."

Looking back to Clark, he raises an eyebrow at me in expectation so I say the only thing I can think of and try to add a little pity-inducing dramaticism, "I wanted to wait until I was broke and jobless, too, so we'd be even, but you went and got a job."

He laughs and looks down at his dirty work boots, "I didn't just get a job, I made my own job." He pauses for a moment, thoughtfully, then looks at Wendy and asks, "Wendy, is Jo the hot girl that you said wouldn't go that week because she was scared of camping in the dark AND couldn't fight her way out of a wet paper bag?"

Now all eyes are on Wendy's embarrassed face and she's the one trying to figure out how to come out on top of the situation. "Errrr, uh-um..."

I fold my arms over my chest and give her the raised eyebrows of expectation. I can half-see Clark, Clarence, and Andrew, out of the corner of my eye, each repeating the gesture in succession.

Shifting her weight to one side and jutting her hip out, she lights her cigarette, takes a drag, and blows the smoke into the air above her head. Leveling her eyes back on us, she says, "Okay, fine, yes, I said that. But! In my defense, Jo kept coming up with excuses and the last one had something to do with being in the woods in the dark. Now will y'all take your disappointed looks and put 'em back in your pockets or wherever you happened to pull them out of?"

I give a little chuckle and realize that I'm the only person that seemed to get what she was just implying. Clark slips his arm out of mine and puts it around my shoulder, "Well, Wend-ers, this little tiger might LOOK like she couldn't fight her way out of a paper bag but I'd bet money on 'er in a title fight."

Wendy looks at me with confusion until Clarence says, "From what I hear, she's gotta hell of a right." Wendy's confusion melts into a look of pride. "My kinda girl. Sounds like we're gonna welcome you to the family!"

Andrew lifts his muscled arm and says to Wendy, "Come here, darling and stand by the fire. Just keep that smoke out of my face. Now, tell me more about you girls in college. Pillow fights, dirty secrets, I want ALL the gossip!"

Wendy and I release each other and look in each other's face as if we might be able to find the answer in each other's eyes. She gives me a conspiratorial look and says, "Well, we had some classes together but didn't really know one another and then we sort of started a book club. Actually, we both had a mutual friend, Macy, that started a book club as an assignment for a class. She had to start some club and work out the dynamics of power so she chose a book club and we were both guilted into being the first members."

"Oh, right, yeah! And I was the one that had to decide what everyone would have to read and what the penalties would be for non-completion and Wendy was the treasurer. We all had to put money in, based on a sliding scale, depending on income, to pay for the books."

"Yep, and then one month, Jo here, felt bad for the girls that had kids and were always broke so she picked up copies of a children's book and five bottles of decent but cheap wine with what was left of that month's book fund. The whole thing fell apart after that. That's why we called her Jo-Nana. To make sure that nobody got a penalty, she read it to us. I still have my copy."

"Oh lord! Please don't tell them that, I hate that name! And, it was six bottles because, if you bought six, you got a discount."

Andrew laughs and says, "I think it's cute! In fact, I think I'll just shorten it to Nana."

"I don't know if I could live with that." I say and laugh. "I think Macy was so mad at me, she never called me by my real name again. I accidentally ruined her project." Looking to Wendy, I ask, "How is she doing, by the way?"

"Oh, Macy? As good or bad as you'd expect for someone in her condition. I think they're going to get a divorce. She completely blames her husband; you remember Travis... Anyway, Mark's in counseling and he's doing better but Macy's just a mess. A total wreck. How come I didn't see you at the funeral."

"Who died?" I ask, in shock.

"You didn't hear? Adam died! Travis swears he had shut and locked the gun cabinet but, somehow, one of the kid's from Adam and Mark's school were able to get in it, they were screwing around and being stupid kids. Adam was accidentally shot between his collar bone and shoulder. I guess it tore open a major blood vessel or something and they couldn't stop the bleeding. You didn't hear about this? He died on the way to the hospital."

"But I didn't DO it!" All eyes, within hearing distance, turn on me as the color drains from my face.

31

After my poorly worded outburst and even poorer attempt to cover it up and back pedal with whatever lame and misleading excuses I could think of, Clark and I left the party before the stroke of midnight came. No matter excuse I had come up or what deviation I thought might seem plausible, I could see the gears turning in everyone's eyes. Doubt and a hidden distrust vaguely showed in the face of anyone that ventured to speak with us. The only one that seemed immune (and maybe even a little empathetic) was Clarence, Clark's brother. Knowing that I might have his empathy or, at the very least, his pity made it better and worse at the same time.

On the drive back to Clark's place, I tried to stare out of the windshield, in front of me, but couldn't help sneaking quick peeks at his face. I was dying to know if he was okay; if we were okay. I half expected him to take a detour to the homeless shelter and dump me on the corner with a promise to deliver my car and clothes with nothing more than a wave goodbye out the window of the truck. Instead, his voice startled me from my thoughts and he asks, "So, I know you probably don't wanna talk about it but I sorta feel like I need to know."

Too terrified to speak a word, I shift my body toward him, in my seat, and look at his face. "What did you mean when you said that you 'didn't do it'?"

Somehow, somewhere in my brain, I knew that question was coming. I try to think back about what I may have told him in regards to my injured hand but I draw a blank. I was raised to always tell the truth, no matter what, but have learned the hard way that I can't always tell the whole truth when it involves episodes. Not wanting the silence to continue for too long, I sigh and say, "Well, it's a little complicated..."

He gives me a brief look and returns his eyes to the icy road while he says, "'It's complicated' isn't going to be able to cut it on this one. What did you do or didn't do? Did you have something to do with that gun cabinet being unlocked?"

An icy chill, that I'm pretty sure didn't come from outside, makes the hairs on my arms stand up and feel my eyes tingling with the threat of tears. I look down at the fingers in my lap and try to control my body's subconscious response to this first sign of distrust. My nose starts to run and I give a pathetic sniffle, silently hating myself for seeming like such a baby. Silent tears begin to roll quickly down my cheeks and my voice cracks a little as I say, "I wasn't really there!"

Clark looks at me and I try to show him my honesty and sincerity by looking him straight in the eyes, waiting for him to tell me that it's over. Instead, his face softens a little and he says, "Hey, it's okay. I didn't mean to upset you. I forgot that she was your friend and you probably knew her kid. I just... Why did you say that you didn't do it? What do people think that you did?"

I try to take a few deep breaths and calm myself before I reply. Clark opens the center console and removes a few napkins from a drive-through. Handing them to me, "Whatever it is, I believe that you didn't do it."

Laughing and feeling a little better now, I say, "Thanks!" and wipe my eyes and nose with the coarse napkin. "But, I wasn't trying to stall, just trying to find the right words, when I said it was a little complicated because it actually is a little complicated.

"Well, I took a nap today so I've got as long as it takes."

I take that as an unspoken leniency to sit and think for a few minutes before I have to respond. *What should I tell him? What CAN I tell him? There's a small chance he'll believe me and an even bigger one that he'll tell me to pack my shit an' git.*

My money's on the latter. He already knows you have problems and a lot of them. He's not going to want to add one more piece of crazy to the puzzle.

If you had just been honest, from the start, he would have been able to help you come up with some sort of cover story when you decided to open your mouth at the party. But you didn't and this is the repercussion for your actions and your dishonesty. He deserves better; to have someone that he can trust. Not just someone that tells him what they think he wants to hear.

If I did tell him, in the beginning, he probably would have left. Am I not allowed to have love, too?

Honestly, is it really love when you don't even give him a chance and you hide half of your life from him? He has no idea what's been going on lately and just how bad shit is. If you really think that you love him, you need to tell him everything and I mean EVERYTHING. There's truth to the saying about setting something free and, if it comes back, and all that. If it wasn't true, it would be a saying.

I look at Clark and he looks back at me. I open my mouth to speak but realize that I still don't know where to start. "I'm sorry. I just don't know where to start."

"Then start at the beginning. Seems like a good enough place. Start with the loaded guns. Start with unsupervised teenagers. Start with how you could possibly 'not really be there'. Because, where I come from, you're either there or not. There is no maybe."

I can sense the tension rising again and I feel the distrust starting to regain ground and I know that I absolutely must find some way to explain or I'll lose him completely. *Start at the beginning,* my inner-voice tells me. *Just go clear back to the very beginning. If he doesn't accept it, there's nothing that you can do but at least he'll know and at least you'll be able to find out if you're destined to be alone for the rest of your sad and pathetic existence until you either die or lose your mind, too.*

I groan and bury my face in my hands as we're pulling onto his street. Realizing that this, too, could be seen as a delaying tactic, I sit up straight and gesture with my palms, toward the roof of the truck. "Well, okay. I'll start at the beginning. But, you'll have to bear with me because you might not understand how it's related but you will when I'm done. You just have to listen. I mean, you can ask questions if you want but it's going to be a slightly long story."

He pulls the truck up, in front of the house and I can't help but notice that he's left more room than usual for me to back out of the driveway. Putting the truck in park, he turns off the engine, grabs the door handle, looks at me, and says, "You start talking and I'll make the coffee."

I can feel that the tension has decreased, ever so slightly, and I force myself to not smile at this little victory. I get out of the truck and take another deep breath before I begin, "Well, you know how I have this... These night terrors, right?"

He looks at me without even trying to hide his confusion and I can see the edge of his lip raise a little and twitch as he wonders how that has anything to do with someone's kid being killed. Quickly, I try to reassure him, "Okay, like I said, it's complicated and this literally is the beginning."

Confusion turns to a slightly less obvious look of concern and he heads toward the house. With an audible exhale and an almost imperceptible shake of his head, he says, "Alright, I'm listening."

32

I had decided that my conscience was right and that honesty was going to be the best policy. No matter how terrified I was of losing Clark, should he not want to accept me after being told everything, I was much more afraid of what could happen if I didn't. He had always been caring and compassionate. He understood me, as much as I would allow, and he had been supportive. If he was anybody that I might not have to see again for a few years, I would have lied. I would have blamed it on the alcohol and mis-hearing what Wendy had said. But, with Clark, if I lied and made up some excuse, years or even months down the road, something could happen again. Who knows how long it could take.

When something else did happen, he would know that there was a problem because this night would always be there, right at the back of his brain, telling his watchers to be on the lookout for danger. He would find out that I was not what I said I was and then happiness would be replaced with anger, trust replaced with the cold realization that nothing I ever said could be counted as true, and every good memory that we might have made together will be tainted for him. Not only would it be difficult to live the guilt of deceiving him (if I lied), but the imminent spiral of our relationship would likely destroy me.

Since Clark has shined so brightly as the one good and steady thing that I could come to hold onto, I cherished that enough to just tell him the truth. I knew that he might not believe me. I knew that he might think that my particular brand of crazy was just too much to handle. And I knew that he might be a little heart-broken if he decided that I was just completely out of touch. I hoped that he would believe me, that he would say he understands, and there was even a wild hope that he would have had similar experiences but I knew that he hadn't. The only real hope that I could hold onto would be that he would not pass judgment but politely inform me that me, my baggage and my belongings, would need to find a new place to stay. As much as I didn't want that to happen, I couldn't avoid the truth that, after analyzing all possible outcomes, this was the most likely.

~~~~

So, I had started at the beginning and told him everything. Everything about the dreams I've had, the people who died, Miles and our forum, even the book in Dr. Marie's office and the chilling correlations of tribal Spirit Walkers to my own life. I even told him about the creepy old man and the scary voice of the woman, that had called me an 'evil, wretched girl', and how I left to find alcohol to knock me out. I had no proof for anything except my emails after events had occurred but I did what I could to convince him. When I had felt like I was reaching the end of my narrative, I pulled out my computer and showed him the first messages between Miles and myself; hoping this would prove that there are others like me and that I'm not nuts. I even offered that it could be argued that Miles was nuts, too, but hoped that the multitude of information might back us up.

When he was done reading, Clark let out a heavy sigh and got up to refill his coffee cup. I watched in silence, tearing the label of my beer bottle, and feeling exhausted and numb. Too numb to even really worry about what was coming next. Once his cup has been filled, he turns back toward me and our eyes meet for a brief moment. I don't know if he looked away because I removed mine first. Anytime that our eyes had met, during my prior explanation, I had the feeling of a spark going off inside of me. Like a lighter that has been flicked but won't light. Making eye contact makes me want to tear that part out of me that causes that feeling.

Looking around the crowded living room at all of my boxes, I was struck by the thought: *If he asks me to leave, I could sleep in a storage unit until I figure something out.*

Clark sits down on the couch next to me and takes a sip of his coffee. Startled, I feel Clark place his calloused hand on my knee and I look back into his eyes but he just stares blankly, into the living room.

Oh, crap, I think I broke him... I take a sip of my beer and try to clear my throat. Attempting a nonchalance tone, I ask, "Are you okay?"

He turns his head and looks down at me but I can't read what's behind his eyes. He ponders the question and I can see that he wants to answer but hasn't quite decided on the words. A tiny light flicks on behind his eyes and his face gets serious, "You haven't had a dream about me, have you?"

With the slightest lift of the weight that has been holding me, I find myself solemnly laughing. I know that I shouldn't be laughing and this is definitely not the time for it so I recover myself and say, "No, not that kind of dream but I do have dreams that you're in sometimes."

"Okay. So, correct me if I'm wrong here but, from what I think I understand, you're saying that you and Miles can... What? Communicate with spirits? Cross over into the spirit world? Is that it?"

Even though I sense no danger in his tone or the way he forms his question, years of experience have taught me that there is danger in the words, themselves. A special sentinel was long ago set up in my brain to watch for certain target words or terms like: you think, you're saying, you believe, etc. I can feel my muscles tense at the recognition that this could be dangerous ground and tell him, "No, I'm not saying that I think or believe any of that. What I'm saying, more than anything, is that Miles and I (and a few others), have been trying to find logical, scientific, real-world answers to what's going on. We've looked at different religions, historical accounts, personal accounts from people online, and are just at the very beginning of putting the pieces together. The problem is, it's like the pieces of one hundred different puzzles, all mixed together, and we're trying to find the pieces that build the picture for our particular puzzle. Does that make sense? I mean, does what I'm saying make sense?"

Scratching his head, he replies, "Well, yeah, I mean I guess. As long you don't think a god is talking to you or that there are angels in your head... Actually, if you ever do come to that conclusion, I'd like to be the first to know."

Noting the softening tension in his neck and jaw and feeling relieved at this small movement back toward normalcy, I laugh a little and tell him, "Actually, speaking of angels. I actually have a funny story. Well, I don't know if it's funny exactly but I've always thought that it was interesting."

Clark checks the clock on his phone and says, "Well, it's a little after midnight and I'm still not tired so let's hear it."

I try to stop my face from showing any signs of disappointment over spending yet another New Years without a kiss at midnight. Looking down into my lap, I twist my hand distractedly around the beer bottle. "Um, well, okay, so, when I was a kid, my great-aunt once told me that freckles were angel kisses. She knew about my night terrors so she told me that the angels could hear me cry and that they would come down and kiss me to make me feel better but that their lips were so hot (because angels are usually on fire) that their kisses would be little dots on my skin." I hold my arm out and show him the numerous freckles and moles that polka-dot my skin. "I completely believed her because, as I got older, I got more. At one point, I was actually afraid that they would make me completely covered and I would turn brown. Being a silly kid, I actually thought that that might be why black people are black."

Chuckling, Clark says, "I'm gonna tell Andrew you said that. He'll get a kick out of it."

Slightly embarrassed, I protest, "But I was just a kid!"

"Nope, telling him anyway."

"Well, in my defense, my grandma also believed in angels. Sometime either before or around the same age, I was at my grandma's house, alone with her. I don't remember why I was there or very much about it but, what I do remember, I believed until I was in my late teens. Then the world sort of beat it out of me and I stopped believing."

Now intrigued, Clark turns a little in his seat and takes a sip of his coffee, looking me in the eye to show his interest. That spark with no light feeling comes again inside my guts and I look away. I take a sip of my beer and continue, "So, anyway, I was really little. I was in my grandma's bedroom. There was a door on the right, a closet next to the door with stuff in it (and I used to be positive that she had just let me out of the closet but I don't know anymore). The bed was in the middle of the room and there was a window in the wall, to the left of the bed. So, my memory is, after grandma released me from the closet, she told me that there were angels watching me and she asked if I could see them. I told her that I couldn't and she said that she could because she had angels, too. She said that the angels talk to us and that she can hear what mine are saying to me. She said it's because we're Indians and we're a special people. Even as a kid, I thought that was a little crazy and I suppose she could see that." I pause for a minute and say, "I'm going to get another beer. Do you want anything?"

"I'm good but, if you wouldn't mind bringing the coffee pot in here, that would be great."

Smiling, I head to the kitchen and wash out my bottle to place it in the new recycle container. I grab another beer and the coffee pot and head back. Placing the coffee pot on my own coffee table (since Clark didn't have one), I move George over a little so that he can't get knocked over by accident.

Reseating myself on the sofa, I continue, "Okay, so, my grandmother says that she's going to show me the angels and prove it. There was a painting, hanging behind us, because she was an artist. She turns me around and says, 'Now watch. You'll see them but, since you're so little, you might only seem them for a second before they vanish.' She quickly lifts the painting from the wall and says, 'Did you see it?' I honestly didn't see anything and had no idea what I was even looking for. I thought she might be joking so I laughed and told her no. She actually looked at me like I had just failed some basic test or like I was an idiot or something. She says, 'Okay, try again but, this time, you need to believe that they're there and you have to make your brain LET yourself see them.'"

I pause and look at Clark to make sure that he's not sleeping or giving me the I'm-gonna-run-now face but he sips his coffee, eyes on mine, waiting for me to continue. "So, right below the painting on the wall are two paintings, leaning against the wall, on the floor. She tells me to get ready and swiftly jerks both paintings forward, away from the wall. Now, I know better now because I'm older but, up until I lost faith in humanity around 18, I would have sworn to any god in heaven that there was a circle of light on the wall. It stayed for maybe a full second (which is actually a good deal of time, if you think about it) and then it shot off to the left, really fast."

"Did your grandmother really believe that stuff?"

"Oh yeah, my grandmother was 'touched'. That's part of why I began to study religion. I thought she was crazy because she actually HAD been touched by the angels. Society, however, has explained that it was not angels but just bad wiring."

33

We spend a little more time on the couch, talking, until about two in the morning. Clark yawns and says that he's ready for bed. Not being able to bring myself to ask if that means that I'm invited, too, I just remain sitting on the couch. He stands up, looks at me, and asks, 'You coming?' Smiling and a little shameful, I admit that I wasn't sure if he wanted me to come or not.

"Well, you've got your pills, right?"

"Actually, I don't know where they are." I look around at the living room and the various boxes before I look back at him. *Honesty is the best policy.* "To be honest, I haven't known where they are for a while now. I thought I'd find them when I was packing but I didn't. My next appointment isn't for another two weeks so I'm not sure that I'd be able to get any, any time soon. I can't even get a refill at the pharmacy because there was a 90 day supply in the bottle and I'd only got it a month ago."

"Well, tomorrow's a holiday but you can call them on Tuesday and see if you can get something worked out. If you can't, maybe we can find a strait jacket, at the second hand store, to lock you up at night."

Even though his comment was light-hearted and meant to convey humor, I don't laugh. I can laugh at a lot of things, myself, my disorder, other people with the disorder, and just other people in general, but I haven't yet accepted who and what I am enough to laugh at that. Clark doesn't even seem to sense that I didn't appreciate the humor so I drop my eyes to the floor and ask, "So, does that mean that we're okay? I mean," (I want to say 'as a couple' but, for some reason, feel it's too presumptuous at this point so, instead, I say,) "The two of us, in our relationship."

The instant change to a look of thoughtfulness tells me that he doesn't want to say what he's about to say and my heart goes into freefall before the words even come out of his mouth. "Well, I'll be honest, Jo. It's kind of a lot to take in and I'd like a little time to think it over."

"Can I ask to which side you're currently leaning?"

That old, beautiful smile returns and I see a little sparkle light up his eyes, and my heart inches its way back up, like a cage-fighter trying to get up after a knock-out. "I'd say the odds are definitely in your favor. I just need a little time to sort it out in my head."

All I can do is nod as I get up from the couch to follow him into the bedroom. I haven't had enough to drink to just pass out but I have had enough to relax. *Who knows, maybe I'll sleep tonight.*

~~~~

The warmth of a late-spring sun radiates off of the gray stones of the house, behind me, and I look out over the lush, green grass of the enormous yard. Breathing in the crisp, fresh air, I smile as the music of birds comes to me from the trees that line the edges of the property. The sun glints off the primary-yellow, plastic roof of a very large playground set about forty yards away, in the grass. The tower, covered red slide, and grounds are empty but inviting. Everything is peaceful and I want to stay in this moment forever.

Turning my head, I look up at the two-story, grey stone house, I tilt my head as slowly look over its face. *I wonder who lives here...* My eyes pass from window to window and a movement catches my eye from the furthest window. Squinting and trying to focus, I lift my hand to my face and block the sun from my eyes. Someone looks back at me from behind the window. Reds, whites, and yellows move around the person but I can't tell if it's curtains or clothing. I can't make out the person's face but I feel an immediate dread and a sense of panic. Still keeping my eyes on the window, I take a few, slow, steps forward, away from the house, in hopes of getting a better view. With my hand still poised to block the sun, I can just make out that it's a man. Something flashes in the bottom, right-hand corner and I back up, further from the house, as a bubbling fear sneaks up my spine.

The man backs up from the window and I see another brief flash before the darkness of the room beyond consumes the vision and the glass reflects the sun again. I search the other upper-stories of the home but see nothing. No movement. I take a several more steps, backwards and away from the house, lowering my hand, as I keep an eye on all of the potential exits. There are no cars or anywhere to really run but I continue to back up and my feet crunch on the dirt and gravel beneath me.

A smear of red and white cloth races passed one of the lower windows on the left side of the house and something glints a flash of light, inside the house. I see the running figure pass by more windows and I fling my eyes to the right side of the lower story until I spot a door. The man is running to the door.

Goosebumps race over my flesh, panic grips my throat, and I know that I need to run. He's coming for me. Every atom in my brain is screaming at me to go! Just GO! But my feet keep me rooted on the edge of the border between the dirt and the grass. The feeling that my brain is moving faster than time kicks in and my eyes widen as I see the door open inward and a man emerges; the vivid colors of his outfit are caught from the corners of my eyes as I turn away. I hear a shrill, piercing, evil scream, and my blood turns cold. Without even thinking, my brain commands the muscles in my legs to prepare for sprint and to bolt so fast that I don't even realize it's happening until I'm already at full speed, running across the grass.

The piercing scream comes again and my heart is about to explode. My ankles slam together during their passing motion and I go down hard, onto my shoulder, rolling forward with the momentum. Desperately clawing at the grass to get myself up and moving again, I look quickly behind me and see the man reaching the edge of the grass. My brain finally registers that he's wearing a white cleaner's outfit with one red and one blue sleeve. His thick face is sickeningly white but not with makeup. Cracked and full lips are open in a grin, showing yellow teeth with jagged points. Unnatural, yellowish-brown eyes bore into mine an evil and a darkness, so complete, that I almost just give up.

Go! Run! Keep going! My inner-voice screams so I get to my feet and run again, heading straight for the massive playground set. *Get on the other side of it! Put it between you and him.*

I apply more pressure to the ground as I launch my strides, trying to gain more distance and reach the wooden support poles of the equipment.

Ducking, I angle my feet and let my momentum slide my feet across the yellow bark chips, under a suspended wooden bridge. I'm not sure exactly how tall he is but I don't think he could get under as easily. Slowing down, on the other side of the bridge, I try to balance myself, to keep from falling, and I look back to see where he is. Somehow, he's gotten much closer and he grins with malice. The fissures in the dry lips tear further open and blood start to leak out of the cracks.

Oh Jesus Christ! I want to scream but am too terrified for any sounds to come out. He's at the edge of the grass where it meets the bark, on the other side of the suspended bridge. I can clearly see now that he's in a homemade outfit, hand sewn; a white jump suit with one bright red arm and one bright blue. Colored poms have been jaggedly sewn over the tops of the buttons. A very deep and maniacal giggle comes out of his chest, shaking his blood red hair. The anxiety of likely defeat pours over me.

Without warning, he lunges forward, under the bridge and I scream and jump as he grabs my ankle. I grab the rope supports for the bridge's railing and pull myself up, as fast as I can, kicking to release my foot from his hold. Getting one foot onto the wobbling, wooden planks, I give another kick and free my other foot. Simultaneously bringing it up onto the bridge, I spread the rope the supports apart and climb through them, landing on the planks with my hands and knees. The scream comes again from underneath me and, without even bothering to gain my footing, I angle my torso toward the landing at the end of the bridge and launch my body as hard as I can.

Gaining the deck, I climb up and hands and feet, up wooden steps to the crow's nest and entrance to the slide. I look down and see the flash of his costume coming up the stairs on the other end of the bridge. *Wait!* My inner-voice says, so I wait. Blood is now trickling down his chin as he grins and shows me the points of saw-like teeth. He twists the butcher knife in his hand to flash the sun off of its blade and slowly begins to walk across the bridge. *Wait!*

His smile grows as he gets closer to the landing at the end of the bridge and I hear the scream come again. I don't know how but I know that it's coming from him. Emanating from him. An unnatural and abhorrent scream of delight. He steps up, onto the landing, and off of the jostling bridge. *Wait!* He takes two steps forward and grabs the railing of the wooden steps, never moving his eyes from mine. Placing one foot on a wooden step of the stairs below me, I take one step backward. The other foot lifts off the landing and comes down on the next step, lifting him up, and I take another step backward. *Wait!* His lower foot lifts and tilts his fiery red hair, eyes still staring into mine, a droplet of blood drips off of his white skin and lands on his raised knee as he places the foot on the next step, climbing higher. Again, I take one step backward. He winks his yellow-brown eye as he lifts the next foot, coming even closer.

Go! I simultaneously spin as I shoot away from him and dive into the top of the slide, turning myself to a seated position as my lunge carries me, twisting, through the brightly lit, red tube. Poised and ready to shoot to my feet and run to the trees, I'm sent through the last turn of the slide and I see the light at the opening. Coming around and ready to run, time slows again as I feel the friction of the tubes plastic, rubbing my legs, the opening of the slide darkens and his face comes into view as the slide fires me towards him.

Scream is the only thing that I can do.

34

I clench my eyes as tight as I can and raise my hands, defensively, in front of my face as I scream. A broken, man's voice comes to me in snatches as I refill my lungs in between screams. The voice is calming and getting louder and I hear, "It's okay... It's gonna be okay. You're here. Everything is fine. Hey, come on, wake up!"

Breathing heavily and fast, my inhales are so sharp that they make a little sound and my throat hurts. Without moving my hands from my face, I raise my eyelids, just a little bit, and see light around me and a rumpled blanket over my legs and I'm sitting up. Opening my eyes a little wider, I look around my arms at the rest of the room and find that I'm in someone else's room and not in my house. Even the blanket isn't mine.

"Are you okay, now?"

I jump my eyes to the location of the voice and see a man, standing in nothing but underwear near an open door. "Who..." I try to speak but it comes out in a croak and my throat burns with the exercise. Swallowing what little saliva I have to soothe my throat, I try again, looking at the man, "Who are you?!"

A mix of scared confusion alters his face and he says, "It's me, Clark! Do you know where you are?"

Puzzled, I think, *Who the hell is Clark? And why is he standing there with nothing but his underwear on?* I look around the room and try to force my brain to start working. Taking in this strange environment, I look down to make sure that I have clothes on and find that I'm fully dressed. My black, spaghetti-string top is stuck to my sweaty chest and back and my jeans feel too tight. As the rush of adrenaline begins to subside, I feel the old, familiar tingling in my veins and I begin to shiver.

"Jo, do you know where you are?"

I look back up at his dark goatee and blue eyes and memories begin to come back. The name Clark belongs to that face, those lips have touched mine, those hands have callouses, and that torso is warm, and those arms are strong when they hold me. Enough information has been released, from whatever door is blocking my memories, for me to feel a sense of security. One of my inner-voices has come back, just enough, to make me aware that silence is not a good thing in these situations and that I need to be careful about what I say. Even though my brain is still muddled, I say, "Yeah, um, we're at your house."

Clark shakes his head and starts to come toward the bed, "Yeah, except it's 'our' house now. Yesterday, you turned over your keys for your old place and came to live with me. We're in my room. Well, our room. Are you okay?"

I nod my head. *I'm definitely better than I would be if I hadn't woken up!* It seems like most of my memories of who I am and where I am have come back and I feel silly for forgetting Clark. *He can't take it personally; I forget who I am all the time!* I still feel like some memories are missing but, without knowing what they are, I can't really know if they were ever there in the first place. It just feels like there are empty spots in my head where something used to be. Like my memory bank has been robbed.

I look back up at Clark and ask, "Would you mind getting me something to drink?"

"What do you want me to get?"

I reach up and massage my throat, "Anything would be awesome! Especially if it's cold."

"Sure thing." He nods as he starts to turn toward the door. Stopping on the threshold, he looks back at me and says, "So, something kinda weird happened. Are you up for going in the living room and talking for a bit?"

"I'm certainly not going back to sleep any time soon so yeah!"

"Okay, then I'm getting a beer. Do you want one?"

The thought of an ice cold beer makes me stickily aware of the sweat that is covering my body and has matted my hair to my forehead. *I must look absolutely terrible!* I wipe my hair off of my forehead and try to smash it down with my hands. "That sounds awesome, actually!"

As Clark turns back to the hallway and heads to the kitchen, I wait until he's a few steps away before I get out of the bed. I quickly change into a big, soft t-shirt and some shorts before sneaking down the hall and into the bathroom to check my hair and make sure that I don't look like a mad woman.

With a little water to tame the beast on top of my head, I wash my face and splash some cold water on my neck and my chest. I hear Clark toss two bottle caps into the trash and he yells, "Ready when you are." One more look in the mirror and I'm fairly confident that I can pass for normal. I head back out and turn into the living room.

"What time is it?" I ask, as I take a beer from his hand.

"It's only a little after three. We were literally only in bed for a little over an hour."

Shame colors my face and I say, "I'm really sorry about waking you up. I know you were tired."

"No, it's okay. And, actually I don't even know if it was you waking me up. I remember dozing off and I was dreaming about a house or something and then there was this scream. It woke me up and scared the sh-crap out of me. It could have been you but I don't think it was. It was like it came from somewhere outside the bedroom. Really freaked me out. Almost like a screech owl but different. And not like your screaming. Your screaming is LOUD! I'm actually a little worried that the neighbors might have heard and called the cops."

I instantly drop my shoulders and smack my head against the back of the couch, "Shit!"

"Um, yeah, I should probably put on some pants, just in case." He sets his beer on the coffee table and stands up. I can't help but admire his muscled frame, regardless of the situation. As he heads back down the hallway, he shouts over his shoulder, "If you see any blue, flashing lights or creepy dudes in costume, just yell."

My eyes widen a little at this odd choice of words but I don't say anything until he comes back, wearing a pair of clean, blue flannel pajama pants. He picks up his beer and sits down. Noticing that I'm staring at him, he says, "What?"

"Hold on!" I say, and jump up from the couch, knocking my knee really hard against the coffee table. George wiggles as if he's laughing at my clumsiness but I try to pretend that nothing happened. I set the beer down on the table and limp toward my boxes, piled at the side of the room.

"Are you okay?" He says laughing.

"Fine, one sec." I locate the box that I had appropriately titled 'writing crap' and move the two boxes stacked on top of it. Opening it up, I find my notepads and pens. Taking two of each, I turn back around to face Clark. "Okay, while it's still fresh in your head, I want you to write down as much detail as you can remember about your dream. I mean EVERYTHING. I'll do the same thing but I'll sit over here, on the floor."

"Why? I could just tell you about it."

"No, I want you to write it. After you do, we'll trade and, if it's not what I'm thinking, I'll explain. If it is, though, I won't have to explain anything and you'll get it."

He sighs and says, "Fine but I'm not a very good writer. Hell, I can hardly even spell correctly."

"Nope, it's fine. Doesn't have to be perfect, just tell me what you saw."

Clark takes the pen and notepad from me and take a seat on the floor opposite him. He gives me one last look and I see the concern from earlier creep into his face. Now, I'm wondering if this was a bad idea but it's too late to stop it so I look down at my notepad and write the highlights from my dream.

It takes me longer than it does Clark and I know that he probably only has a few sentences but I'm not too worried. *Okay, moment of truth. Let's see what he's got.* I stand back up and hand him my notepad and take his. Instead of returning to the floor, I sit next to him and read what he has written:

> This is silly but here goes. Grey house made out of rocks. 2 stories. Lots of windows. Grass, trees, playground equipment. Someone in the house on the top floor. Weird costume. Very creepy. Woke up to screaming sound.

Even with my shock, the snide voice in my head says, *No wonder it didn't take him very long to write it.* I look at Clark and study his face. With every word that his eyes cross over, they grow wider and wider. Without removing his eyes from the page, his brows furrow and he tries to speak, "How-- What the hell?!" He continues moving his eyes down the page until he reaches the end. He looks up at me with shock and confusion, the color drained from his face. "How is this possible?"

35

Clark and I talked until almost dawn but only had one more beer a piece as we waited for the coffee pot to finish brewing. I explained to him that I have no idea how it was possible to have the same dream as someone else but that this wasn't the first time that it's ever happened. With humility and a touch of embarrassment, he apologized for his behavior and distrust from earlier in the night. I admitted that I had actually debated telling the truth or lying to him when he asked for my explanation of what I'd said at the party. He assured me that he was very glad that I'd told the truth because, he said, I'd make a terrible liar.

I couldn't help but laugh on the inside at that statement because the truth was that I've been forced to lie to people for my entire adult life. When you show up for work, haggard and with black circles under your eyes, people think you're weird if you tell them that you couldn't sleep because you had a nightmare. I've had to get very creative with my explanations but I didn't want Clark to potentially add this information to his memory for later use.

He went back to bed at a little after five, kissing me on the forehead, and saying that he was sorry, again. As I watched him head back to the bedroom, I smiled and thought to myself, *Last year ended really crappy but today is a new year and it's going to be the best year I've probably ever had!*

~~~~

I wake up to Clark gently shaking my leg while a loud buzzing sounds, intermittently, from somewhere in the middle of the room. Sleepy and not ready to wake up yet, I struggle to open my eyes, happy that I can immediately recognize his voice.

With mock annoyance, I whine, "What do you want?! I'm sleeping here!"

He laughs and says, "Your phone has been buzzing for the past hour. I didn't answer it but your caller ID says Noel. She keeps calling so I thought you might want to wake up in case it was an emergency."

My eyes fly open at the thought of Noel. *I didn't even get a chance to tell her I was moving! She probably thinks I died or skipped town on her!* "Oh crap!"

Clark grabs the phone off of the coffee table and hands it to me. He lifts my legs up, from the couch and sits down, putting my, still outstretched, legs on his lap. My phone stops buzzing before I can get my fingers to swipe to answer it. He takes a sip of his coffee and I see him pointing at a fresh, steaming mug on the coffee table.

I swipe at the phone and finally get it to register that I want the home menu. I tap the button for recent calls and tap for it to dial Noel's number. As the device works out my commands, I reach over to pick up the coffee and hear the other end ring.

"Haaaa-llo?"

A little confused and not sure of just who I'm talking to, I say, "Um, hi, this is Jo."

In a slurring, sing-song voice, I hear Noel say, "Oh! My darling Johanna! Oh, how I've missed thee!" A gagging, dry retch follows after

Concern starts to gather in my brow and I say, "Noel? Are you okay?"

"Oh, me? Yeah, no, I'm great. Just great. Fan-fun-tabulous..." I could tell that she was not, actually, great but that something was definitely wrong. I turn to Clark and give him a wide-eyed look of serious concern. Understanding my face, he immediately sits forward on the couch. *Ready for action. What a man!*

The conversation that I once had, with the voice named Amanda at the Suicide Prevention Hotline, flashed through my mind and, with lightning speed, my brain worked out a plan for the conversation. "Noel, are you safe?"

Her tiny voice tinkles with laughter and she says, "Safe?! Is anyone ever safe? You're not safe, I'm not safe, Steve's not safe, nobody's safe!"

Who's Steve? "Can you tell me where you are?" I look at Clark and give him a little gesture of turning a key in my hand. He jumps up, puts his coffee cup on the table, and goes in search of keys.

"I am where I always am. Where I've always been." Her voice drops to that of a sad or frightened child, "And, Jo, I don't like it here anymore. It's sad and it's scary here and I jus' wanna go back to the old place."

"Okay, that's okay. It's okay to feel sad and scared. The world can be a scary place. Are you at home?"

Her voice slurs as she says, "I-I-I-I jus' told you I was at home. Where else'd I be?"

"Okay, I guess I didn't catch that. So, you're at home. Are you alone? Are your parents there?"

"Pshhhhh! Are they ever here? Ha! I think they're gone. Gone far away as possible."

"Noel, have you been drinking anything or taken any medicines or drugs?"

A laugh explodes into my ear and I have to pull the phone away from my face until it dies down into a giggle. She says, "HAVE I?! Yer funny! You always was funny—No... I mean, yes. YES! My step-mom gave me my medice-sis-inal beverage when I was sleeping and tol' me that they had to go but there's a whole bottle of sleepy time shtuff that would make me feel better." I'm up, off the couch and motioning for Clark to hurry up and get the door locked so that we can go get into the truck. Noel's voice comes in rapid fire, "So, I drank it." A hurling noise and gushing sounds immediately follow her statement.

"Noel? Are you okay?" A coughing and another hurling sounds comes.

"Yeah… Wait, no. No, I'm not okay. I'm bleeding, like, from inside my mouth, but I'm okay." I snatch the notebook from last night, off of the coffee table, and furiously scribble as Clark looks over my shoulder: Call 911 - Possible overdose - 2212 Bennett - Get in the truck. He snatches up his phone and his keys as I'm already running out the door to the truck.

As I climb in the passenger seat and give Clark a scared look throught the windshield with the motion to hurry his ass up, Noel continues, "I went to your house last night, to see you, but there was nobody there and somebody took your stuff. I've been trying to call you…"

My heart sinks and I let the muscles in my torso and neck go slack; my head slams against the dash. Clark looks over at me in surprise as he starts the truck and stomps on the gas pedal.

"I know, I know. I meant to call you but I had to move really fast and I was so busy." *Jesus, what a lame excuse. I knew there was something wrong but I was TOO busy.* I raise myself back up in the seat and slap my hand to my forehead, feeling, as I do so, that what I really deserve is a punch in the face.

"Nah, no, is'okay, s'okay. I wasn't ready then anyways. But! I'm ready now. Can you come and take me?" Another, wet, retching sound comes through the phone and I hear her moan.

Oh god, ready for what? "I'm on my way, Noel, I'll be there soon. Don't drink anymore! Don't drink anything at all!"

I whisper to Clark, "On my old street, the blue two story on the corner, HURRY!" He nods a silent affirmation and I say, "Noel? Are you still there?"

"Yip! I'm still here. But not for long, right? I'm gonna make some tea. My dad left me a tea bag on my dresser with little hearts. Idn't that sweet?" Happily, she adds, "I'm not goin' anywhere because you're coming to take me!"

"Where do you want to go? We'll go anywhere. Just tell me where you want to go and don't drink anything."

Ignoring my question, she says, "Yer gonna take me to my mom, right? 'Cause you know where the shadow boy lives, right?"

Fear- complete and total fear- shuts off my eyesight, my sense of touch, and even my sense of being for a few moments... "Why do you think I know where he lives?"

"'Member how I tolds-jou about my mom and the little boy?"

"Yes, I remember. Please don't drink anything. Go outside, Noel, we're almost there."

"Welp! When my mom was on fire and burning and she was dying, right before she fell over and fell down, that little shadow boy tried to help me. He came to me and I thought he was going to help me up. My mom was waving her arms, all crazy-like, when she came falling down. The boy... Well, not really a boy, it wasn't a boy, it was a shadow boy..." She trails off and I hear water running and metal clinking on porcelain. Another heaving sound makes the tears start to form in my eyes

"NOEL!! DON'T DRINK ANYTHING! Don't MAKE ANYTHING! Just get OUT of the house!" Turning to Clark, I yell, GO FASTER!"

He motions to the car-packed road, in front of us and shakes his head, saying, "I can't! It's a big truck but not a Monster Truck! I can't just drive over the cars!"

Angry and not thinking clearly, I widen my eyes even further and yell, "Just do it anyway!"

Noel's voice invades my ear as she says, "I don't think he was s'posed to do it but he did it."

"What did he do, Noel? Noel, please go outside! Go outside and wait for me."

"Nah, I jus', I jus' want some tea. Chai tea is my favorite! So, when my mom fell down, it sorta happened in slow motion, ya know? She was reaching out for the shadow boy, like trying to grab 'im."

"Oh god..."

I realize she hasn't really been listening to me at all and she continues, "She was reaching out for him but, before she got to him, he touched me but I don't think he was s'posed to do that. I'm ready for you, now. That's how I know what you are and that yer gonna take me to see my mommys. I think I can see you. I'm ready for you now... Hey, when we get there, do you think that we could—"

A brief and loud bang exploded in my ear for less than a split second and the line went silent. "Hello? Hello?! Noel!   Noel, are you there?!" My entire body begins to shake with adrenaline and my blood is on fire. "GO! GO! GO!" I yell at Clark, "Drive through the fucking lawns if you have to!"

He looks at me with concern and a little frustration, "Calm down! I'm sure it will be okay! Call her back. Maybe her battery died. She's been calling you all morning!"

I take a full, sharp breath and exhale noisily. I redial Noel's number but it just rings. I hang up and try again, this time it says, "The wireless subscriber, you are trying to reach, is not in..." I hang up and try again but get the same message.

"Shit-shit-shit!"

"What's going on? What happened?"

"I think she's dead! Oh god!" The little sentinel, that keeps an eye over what I say to people or how I act, sounds a tiny alarm and reports, *It's time to breathe. He doesn't know what happened. He doesn't know about Noel, and the fire, and her weird parents, and her being sick. He doesn't know and you need to be careful!* I try to breathe as I'm instructed and watch the cars in front of us. A green Buick, two cars ahead, slams on its brakes, stopping all cars behind, and just lingers in the road.

Move, move, MOVE! As if my inner-voice has reached the old lady driving the Buick, she flips on her turn signal for one second and pulls to the left when there is a break in the line of on-coming traffic. The car behind her, pulls ahead slowly, and begins to pick up speed, only to flash it's brake lights like it's having an aneurism. It inches to the right and it's finally clear that it's pulling into a driveway. Frustrated and driven into a frenzy, I hear myself yell, "MOVE! You FUCKER!"

Clark jumps a little, in his seat, at my unusual use of such profanity but I'm too worried to pay him too much attention. I swipe the screen to dial Noel's number again but get the same message that the subscriber is unavailable. Fresh tears overtake my dry eyes and I look at Clark, "I think she's dead. I don't know if she killed herself or if they killed her but I think she's dead."

"Hey, hey, hey, calm down, I'm sure she's fine. You won't be any help if yer worked up and excited, when we get there."

"Okay," I breathe. "You're right. You're right. I need a solid state of mind in case she needs me and she's not dead yet." I exhale as I lower the window. The sound of sirens reach my ears. *There must be a fire somewhere...*

I recognize that we are on the last street before we turn onto my old street and that Noel's is close to the corner. Desperately wishing that a Godzilla or MegaTron would come to smash down the houses between my view and her place, I watch as a fire truck pulls onto the street, ahead of us.

The cars are slowed with rubber-necking, gawking, and trying to avoid colliding with the lit-up emergency vehicles, as they rush up the street, behind the firetruck and I finally realize what they're here for. "Oh shit, oh shit!"

Clark leans forward in the driver's seat, trying to see around the cars, as he eyes the house where the fire truck has stopped, smoke beginning to billow onto the street. "Oh shit is right!"

Clark pulls onto the road, stopping in the middle of the street, trying not to run over the gawkers that are exiting their vehicles. Smoke pours out the front window and a flame is greedily licking the left side of the house. I jump out of the truck and, without even closing the door, run to the house, screaming, "NOEL! NOEL I'M HERE!"

A big man in a full, yellow uniform, grabs me and stops me from getting too close to the front door, exhaling it's black smoke into the yard.

"You can't go in there!"

Desperately, I try to wrench myself from his iron grip and shout, "NOEL! Noel, I'm here! Come out! I'm here!" The firefighter, lifts me up, off of my feet and begins to walk back across the lawn, as if I'm no heavier than a head of lettuce. Crying and punching him, I lose all sense of normality, shouting and screaming. Hhe sets me down on the grass, at the edge of the lawn as Clark walks up. He slackens his grasp and I bolt for the door, screaming, "I'm here, Noel! Come out! The firefighters are here! Don't stay in there! You don't WANT to go!"

A different firefighter tackles me to the concrete steps, bear-hugging me in an iron grip. Lifting me up, tears fill my eyes and I can't see in the house. He drags my feet across the grass and says, "You CAN'T go in there! You'll die, too!"

The recognition of the word 'too' and its implications shuts down whatever part of my brain controls my body and my muscles. I go limp and mumble teary protestations, with eyes burning from the smoke, I feel myself being lifted and passed into the arms of another, very strong man. A racking noise erupts from my throat as I cry out, one more time, "NOEL!"

36

Clark, diligently, brought home a newspaper every single day, shirking work, and checked the news sites and obituaries for something, anything. I spent every single day, sleeping, balled up on the couch; except for when Clark woke me to make me eat some dinner. Every single night, I had a bloody mary, a whiskey, or a beer in my hand until I could black out.

I didn't call Dr. Marie or search further for the missing pills because my next appointment was set for the following Thursday. I wanted the escape that might come with taking the pills but, something inside of me convinced me that I didn't deserve it. I deserved to suffer in the darkness for awhile.

I didn't reach out to Miles, call him, text him, or even read his emails. I just hoped that he would understand when I did get around to finally telling him what had happened. We had both experienced some awful things (in the real world and that other one) so days of silence weren't all that concerning. The only real concern would be a silence of over a week. Silence lasting that long would most likely mean that the quiet party had succumbed to their demons.

I knew that Noel was dead because I didn't get there fast enough to save her. It was because I didn't do anything about my thoughts or feelings about what might have been going on. Because I didn't man up to my own fears and concerns and just take my damn pills or buy the melatonin and try to get on a normal sleep cycle. *Normal people would have been up before eleven and answered the phone. If I were normal, I could have saved her. If I were normal, I would have done something or said something. If I were normal, she would still be alive.*

My thoughts and theories were proven valid when Clark, apologizing as he came into the living room, handed me a page of the newspaper that he'd been reading in his room. A picture, of a younger and happier Noel, graced the page about a third of the way down. The obituary read that a troubled girl left behind a grieving father and step-mother but would be joining her, already passed, biological mother and older brother, Stephen; and that she would surely rest in peace in such good company.

Floored at the idea that Noel would have an older brother that I'd never even heard about, I re-read the article, a few more times, before her voice echoed in my head, 'Is anyone ever safe? You're not safe, I'm not safe, Steve's not safe, nobody's safe!'

There was a viewing, set for tonight, but I couldn't bring myself to face Noel's soul-less body and I admitted my feelings to Clark. 'I understand.' He'd said. He left for the store, shortly afterward, and returned with a double-sized bottle of sweet, white wine and two massive rib-eyes. This small but thoughtful gift brought me a little happiness and a little light into my dark place, and I thought, *Wow! Wine AND a rib-eye? Boy, does he know how to lift a spirit.*

An uncomfortable feeling, as if I'd just spoken ill of the rising dead, overtook me and I recognized my insensitive choice of words. The realization that I'm a terrible person brought me right back down again.

~~~~

Sneaking into the funeral service because we're late, the next day, I hold Clark's arm with a titanium grip. He had joked about leaving me, during the service, to go get some chicken, or take up smoking again, or just ruminate in silence on his future goals in life but I provided enough of a threat that he decided not to leave me.

In no uncertain terms, did I lead him to believe that, leaving my side, on this day of days, would eventually culminate into his leaving my side forever; willing or not and not necessarily alive, either. I knew I was taking a gamble on the words but it felt important to stand up for who I was and what I had to offer him (little, though it may have been); in sight of Noel's most complete, and utter, sacrifice.

A few friends, but mostly family, took the pulpit to talk about what a troubled girl she had been since the accident with her mother. People described her as dark, melancholy, and sad; I couldn't help thinking that these people obviously never really knew the poor girl but stopped myself from saying anything when my brain reminded me, *These 'people' knew her longer than you did and probably knew her better than you.*

But, still, the urge to say something occupied my brain until the end of the service. When the pastor gave the last call for anyone to speak, I jumped slightly in my chair but settled back against Clark's arm, surveying the improperly dressed crowd that were 'mourning' in ripped jeans and t-shirts.

We exited the funeral home and climbed into the truck as Clark asks, "Do you want to go to the grave-side service?"

"Yes. Yes, I'd like to be there for her." I don't extrapolate on my feelings but I'm sure that Clark can understand why I feel this way.

We drive, in silence, across town, following the vehicles holding immediate family, as they follow the hearse. I tell Clark, "You have to turn your lights on."

"Huh? What lights?"

"Your headlights."

"But it's the middle of the day!"

"I know but it's customary. Please turn on your headlights. It lets the other drivers know that we're a part of the procession." Without a word, Clark clicks the knob, to turn the truck's lights on, and we drive in silence, for the rest of the trip, to the cemetery.

Exiting the truck, we step onto the soft, wet grass of the cemetery, and head toward the PVC-pipe supported tent where Noel's family is gathered. I see a man and woman, that I would bet money, is her father and step-mother, shaking hands with people as they come toward the casket. Two rows of cheap, plastic chairs are set up in front of the ornate, cherry-wood casket, hovering on rails above a hole in the ground Some old, some middle-aged, and one or two younger people take up the front seats, while the rest of us stand. A very old woman blinks her eyes but registers nothing as she sits, in a wheelchair, and has the drool wiped off of the corner of her lips, by a woman, maybe twenty-years younger..

At the sight of the casket, a fissure erupts in the middle of my brain and I think, *I've got to get her out of there! She'll be buried alive!*

No! She's already dead. That's a dead body in that box and you don't want to open it; even if you could.

The pastor, from the funeral home, starts to talk about his god's 'will' and his god's 'plan'. How all the little children must be sent to Him and that there is a place in his heaven for those that were 'touched' like Noel. Fury at his seemingly insensitive words causes me to start forward but the strong arms of Clark hold me back. I desperately want to say something but know that this is certainly not the time or the place.

Once the pastor is finished, the ornate box is lowered into the dark hole. People are invited to grab a mound of dirt, say a prayer for Noel's soul, and toss it onto the polished wood. Clark and I place ourselves toward the end of the line and slowly move forward in the procession so that I can pay my respects the corpse inside the box. Tears start to form in my eyes but I tell myself not to cry. With an incredible bite, the snide voice in my head snarls out, *Saying, 'I'm sorry', now, won't do any good! You should have been there! May as well cry. You're selfish and childish and you were too late when she needed you!*

Coming up to the casket, I try to put these thoughts out of my head and stop the spread of a guilty blush from completely taking over my cheeks. Tears begin to fall and I quickly wipe them away. I pick up a handful of dirt with my wet hands and bits of it turn to mud. I open my mouth to whisper my apologies but an old woman's voice, from the tent area stops me short...

"You're that evil girl" I stop, recognizing this voice from somewhere in my memory. Turning my face to the tent, I look out, over the gathering, searching for the owner of the voice.

"She did it!" I hear, and point my eyes in the direction of the scratchy old voice. "She's the girl that took my Jimmie! She TOOK him!!" My eyes find the mouth from which these protestations came and I see that it's the drooling woman in the wheelchair. Her younger care-taker looks at me, with an instant malevolence, as she tries to soothe the old woman with calming words and tones; but the old woman won't be calmed. Pointing at me and still drooling, she yells, "That's the demon that took my Jimmy! I saw her! Arrest that girl!"

Gasps of shock and surprised sadness overcome the crowd and every eye that turns on me chips away a little bit of my hardened exterior until the light starts to fade, in front of my eyes, and my fingers start to tingle and my arms go numb. Completely mortified and feeling that I must be guilty of whatever crime the Alzheimer's patient says I did, I feel Clark's hand grip me as my muscles begin to give way, under the weight of my own body.

The woman shrieks again, louder, and one last time, "I tell, you, that's the girl that killed my husband!"

The younger woman focuses the power of her hate and disgust, through her eyes, in my direction as she says, "No, Nana. Papa had a heart attack. Nobody killed him. It's okay."

Clark's arms completely encompass me and I feel myself being hauled, swiftly, across the grass and away from the staring eyes of people that I don't know. I see the line of cars getting closer and Clark's truck getting nearer. I feel Clark's arms still holding me, lifting my legs up and feet off the ground. Clark shuffles his arms to free a hand and opens the door of the truck and I faint.

Coming to in the truck and still a little woozy, I ask, "Are we leaving?"

"You bet yer sweet little ass we're leaving. Pitchforks were comin' out!"

Totally confused now, I look at him and realize we're already on the road and driving. "Pitchforks? What are you talking about?"

Completely ignoring my question, he looks, with complete seriousness and gravity, into my eyes, ignoring the road and traffic on the other side of the windshield, and he says, "What's it gonna take to get this forum of yer's up an' runnin' to find more people?"

37

A Little Over One Year Later...

Waking from an afternoon nap in our new bedroom, I hear Clark breath and I smile. The sound of yapping from the neighbor's recent litter of puppies comes through the window behind us. All of our things are still in boxes and, what had been cluttering the living room, was now moved into the bedroom, to make way for the company that we would be having. Between his job and my work on the forum, we hadn't really gotten the unpacking under control even though we'd been living here for three weeks already.

Clark moans a little and turns over to face me, his eyes still closed. A warm happiness floods my heart and I think about waking him up since it's about time to go. We're picking Miles up from the airport and then having an all-out house warming party with Clark's mom, dad, step-mom, and his brother Clarence and his partner Andrew. I had a few family and not-so-close friends that I could have invited but, since Miles was coming, we had agreed to keep the invitations to a strictly 'in-the-know' guest list.

Carefully and slowly, I reach behind me and pick up my phone from the nightstand to check the time. We still have twenty minutes before we need to leave so I set it down, next to me on the bed, and watch Clark.

A smile begins to creep over his face and he wiggles his head on the pillow. "If you don't stop that, you're going to make us late." He says, groggily.

Laughing and surprised that he was already awake, I ask, "Stop what?"

"You know what I'm talking about." He opens his eyes and gives me that look that says he's 'in the mood'.

"No, I really don't know what you're talking about. I was just checking my phone. See?" I sit up on one elbow and show him my phone.

He looks at me a little confused as he says, "You were touching my leg..."

"No, I was not touching your leg. See?" He looks at the hand holding the phone and my bent arm, holding myself up, under the pillow. Pausing for a moment, his eyes widen with concern and, in one, swift, movement, he flings the covers off and jumps, backwards, out of the bed, standing in his underwear.

Startled, I ask, "What's wrong? Is there a bug in the bed or something?" At my own question, I get a little nervous so I get out of the bed, too.

Clark, staring at the blankets, says, "Were you touching me with your feet?"

"No, Clark, I swear! I wasn't touching you at all. You were on the other side of the bed until you rolled over. I couldn't reach your leg without getting up!"

I can see the gears turning in his head as his face goes momentarily white. Shaking his head a little, he says, "It's nothing. I must have been asleep and didn't realize it. I could have sworn there was a hand on my thigh. You swear you didn't do it."

Feeling a little freaked out myself but finding humor in his fear, I can't help but laugh a little and tell him, "I swear, I didn't touch you!"

"Then why are you laughing? The guilty ones always laugh!"

Giggling even more now, I say, "I can't help it, you're just funny when you're scared."

"Oh, I'm funny when I'm scared? Let's see how much you like it if I laugh at you the next time you get one of your visitors. You'll be flailing around in the dark and I'll just be layin' over here laughin' at you." He sounds serious and maybe a little offended but I can tell that he's over it.

"If you do that, I'll tell them you want a hug in the middle of the night."

His face goes blank and his eyes widen, with mock horror, he says, "Please don't do that!"

Laughing more now than ever, I can't get control of my voice as I watch him fling the covers from one side of the bed to the other, searching for his mysterious assaulter. Coming around to my side, he flings them back again, finding nothing. Looking back at me, he says, "You think that's funny, huh?"

Gaining control of myself, I try to give him a look of mock seriousness, "No! Not at all. It's not funny."

Eyeing me suspiciously, he goes back to his side of the bed and locates his pants. "Alright, then. You'd better not laugh at me or I'll dunk you in the snow, on the way to the truck."

The thought of being submerged in the last snows of February sobers me up and I say, "Nope, I'm done laughing. You won't hear another peep from me. Well, unless it happens again." Clark just eyes me, with pretend anger, over his shoulder as he slides his feet into his boots. Taking this as my cue to get ready, I grab my sweater and slip it on. Before switching my slippers for my own boots, I head to the bathroom to check my reflection.

Everything looks to be in order so I head back to the bedroom and find that Clark has vacated it for the warmer comforts of the living room. Rounding the doorway, I see him, standing by the wood stove, sipping a cup of coffee as he surveys the room for any last details we need to wrap up before the party.

"Are you ready to go?" I ask.

"Yeah, I think so. Do you wanna grab a cup of coffee to take with you? I can go start the truck while you fill a mug."

"Sure. I'll see you out there in a minute." We meet in the middle of the living room and give each other a quick kiss on the lips before he turns and heads out the door. I head to the kitchen and fill a travel mug to the brim. Putting the coffee pot back, I grab a lid and sip the liquid from the rim of the cup to prevent an overflow when I put the lid on.

Once out the front door, I lock it behind me and head toward the running truck but see that Clark isn't in the cab. I stop in the middle of the walk-way and look around; half expecting a surprise snow-ball attack. Men's voices come to me between the sounds of kibble being poured into metal bowls for happy puppies. I turn and see Clark, talking to our new neighbor and holding a pup.

I walk through the snow covered yard, smiling in expectation of taking a minute to play with the dogs before we head to the airport. About six feet away from the kennel, I see the puppies, clamoring over one another to get to the food bowls, their mom, or the heated water bowl. One puppy sits still and looks straight at me, a black German Shepherd with caramel-colored paws.

Someone, somewhere in my head finds his place in a memory that I can't conjure and my eyes widen as I say out loud, "It's Zeus!"

THE END

ABOUT THE AUTHOR

Lacy Sereduk-Mitchell is an Idaho native and lives with her husband, their four children, two dogs, two goats, and two chickens. She has been a sufferer of night terrors since birth and wrote <u>Discernment</u>, her first novel, in hopes that it might release some of the pent up frustrations of living with the disorder.

The difficulties faced by the title character, Johanna, in <u>Discernment</u> and <u>D2: Touched</u>, are very real and very well understood by those that can't sleep at night and are, sometimes, even haunted by their disorder by day. She sincerely hopes that, releasing the story of Jo into the world, more people will come to understand and, more importantly, empathize with those that are forced to 'operate outside the time clock' of the general world.

Book three, in the series, is in development so feel free to check out or follow the author's blog at lacysereduk.wordpress.com